OLD HABITS

A SCOTT MARSHALL THRILLER

JOHN CARSON

DI FRANK MILLER SERIES

Crash Point
Silent Marker
Rain Town
Watch Me Bleed
Broken Wheels
Sudden Death
Under the Knife
Trial and Error
Warning Sign
Cut Throat
Blood from a Stone
Time of Death

Frank Miller Crime Series – Books 1-3 – Box set

MAX DOYLE SERIES

SCOTT MARSHALL SERIES

Old Habits

OLD HABITS

Created with Vellum

For my family;
Rich, Steve,
Tammy, Terri, Kathy,
and their families

ONE

If I hadn't answered the phone back then, I wouldn't have died three times. But I had and I did.

Now I'd answered it again, and not for the first time that day, I wondered if I would die again.

I stood looking at the Newburgh Beacon Bridge, spanning the Hudson River, from my vantage point in Hudson Valley College. Sweat was lashing off me, being soaked up by the t-shirt I wore, and I was looking at my smart watch to see if my heart was going to slow down or explode.

'Morning, professor,' one of the security guards said as he pulled up in one of the small SUVs they ran around in. 'Bit hot for running, isn't it?'

'It helps clear the mind,' I said as the man got out of the car. 'You should try it.' He was an ex-cop, like most of the security guys here, and had the physical appearance of a cop with a lot of experience under his belt.

'Wasn't it Noel Coward who sang about Mad Dogs and Englishmen? You ain't English, are you?'

'Not the last time I checked. But I think there's some Irish in there.'

'Isn't there always?' He laughed as he walked into the library.

My breathing slowed down and then I could feel the pain starting to get a grip of my right knee. I told people I fell down some icy steps a few years back and dislocated it. The truth was, a serial killer had kicked my knee out, just before he shot me five times.

The reason the voice in my head was nagging me again.

My FBI colleagues at the time told me it was Tom Morgan. They found him dead an hour later, with the gun still in his possession. He died almost sixty minutes after I died for the first time in the back of the ambulance. He knew they were coming for him, so he'd taken his own life. *Suicide by self-inflicted gunshot wound* the medical examiner put on the death certificate and the grand jury had agreed. Case closed. The man the press had dubbed *The Gravedigger* was having his own grave dug for him.

Despite the heat, I felt chilled inside. My heart rate was coming back to normal. I looked at my watch and

2

the time showed I was five minutes late for my meeting. I turned and jogged down the stairs that led to Columbus Hall, a modern building built in the grounds of what was once a nunnery. I nipped into the restrooms to throw water on my face and dried it off with paper towels. I didn't look my best, but it wasn't as if I had anybody at home to impress.

Students were mostly gone for the summer, although a few were there for summer classes. I knew one or two of them and they said hi to me.

Apart from the theater, offices, and classrooms, there was a small café downstairs called *Washington's*, outside *The Hudson View* restaurant.

This is where Detective Danielle Fox was waiting for me.

She looked fabulous in a white shirt and tan shorts. Her hair was blonder than I remembered it, as if she'd finished it off with a bottle. Her smile was welcoming but with a little added nervousness thrown in for good measure.

'You're looking good, Scott.'

'Thanks. You are too.'

And it was true. I hadn't seen her in three years, not since the first anniversary of what had gone down in her little town. The year I went back, looking for answers, finding none. Now I looked like I'd just swum over the Hudson to meet her, the edges of my hair still damp.

'I feel overdressed,' she said, maintaining her smile as she stood up and held out her hand. I gently gripped it and smiled back, although I didn't feel like smiling. She wasn't here to invite me to a party.

'You're fine. Can I get you anything?' I looked at the bottle of water on her table, sitting next to her sunglasses. Noticed there weren't any cookies or cakes.

'No thanks, Scott, I'm okay.'

I took a bottle of water from the fridge and made small talk with the woman behind the counter as she counted out my change, before joining Dani at the table.

'Please excuse the way I'm dressed. I go jogging, even in this heat, to try and keep the strength up in my knee. My dog prefers to stay in front of the air conditioner.'

'Oh, you have a dog? Boy or girl?'

'His name's Atticus. He's a German Shepherd.' I stopped short of taking my phone out and showing her one of the goofy photos I was always taking of him: standing with his front paws on the back of the couch, barking at the school bus as it stopped to pick up my neighbor's kids; lying on his back in the middle of the living room floor with his tongue hanging out, watching TV upside down; wearing the birthday hat on his first birthday. He was my boy. I wasn't going to let him down. Unlike another special person in my life who I *had* let down.

My phone stayed in my pocket. Just like co-workers who bring in holiday photos of their kids, they only meant something to me.

We both knew we were skirting round the subject, like an awkward couple who want to dance with each other at a school prom but each one is waiting for the other to make the first move.

So I asked her to dance.

'You found her, didn't you?'

I hadn't noticed the briefcase at her feet before, but she brought it up onto the table and put it beside our plastic bottles. Double click and it was open. She took out a folder, as if she hadn't heard my question or was deliberately ignoring it.

'We're not sure.' She slid the folder over to me and put the briefcase back on the floor.

This wasn't the answer I was expecting. It was a straightforward *Yes* or *No*. There should be no ambiguity. It was the reason she'd called me that morning, asking to meet me. Wasn't it? I hesitated for a moment, as if the buff colored folder was really a python in disguise, and she was trying to trick me into touching it so it could strike.

Then I opened it and took out the first photo.

The woman sitting up in a gazebo at the edge of a lake. It was obvious she'd been covered in a homemade shroud, just like the victims from four years ago. Back then, there were six victims in total but he had only dumped two of them. This time, the shroud was over her knees, like a blanket to keep her warm. It was her face that I focused on. It was clear that she'd been dead for a long time, the ground having taken its toll.

'It was taken three days ago,' Dani said.

'Jesus.' I looked at her, knowing I had to ask, not wanting to hear the answer. 'Are you sure it's not her?'

'It's too early. The medical examiner is looking right now.'

I let out a breath, trying not to make it sound like a sigh of relief, but I took a sip of water, just in case my voice croaked. *FBI Agent Jessie Kent. Abducted by serial killer Tom Morgan. Missing, presumed dead. My partner. The woman I had let down four years ago.*

'Any clue as to which one it is?' I said, my voice not letting me down.

'We're still trying to ID her. We'll get there, we just haven't got the results back yet.'

'Any of the others?'

She took some of her own water. It left a fine line on her upper lip. 'No,' she answered.

'Where did this one come from?'

'We're not sure. As you know, Tom Morgan died

before we could find out where he had kept them hidden.'

'And now somebody else has found them and thinks it's fun to display them.'

'We don't know if all of them have been found, or if some sicko just found one and put her on display. That's why I wanted to talk to you.'

'You're looking for a profile from me, and I don't think I can be of any help to you.'

'The Bureau won't help. The case is closed. We got the guy four years ago. Now we're looking for somebody else, so they've washed their hands of it. I thought you'd maybe be able to give us an insight.'

Able to or want to? They were two entirely different questions. Of course, I'd be able to, but did I want to dredge up the memories of that time spent in a no-name town miles from anywhere?

Do it for Jessie. The thought nagged me and I knew that was the road I was going to go down. *Because she hasn't been taken home yet.*

'I'll give it some thought.'

'Thank you, Scott. I knew you would.'

'You could have asked me on the phone when you called me. So, I have to surmise that there's another reason you drove three hours to talk to me face-to-face.'

She smiled a tired smile, as if sleep had eluded her

for the longest time. *Sweet dreams that had turned into nightmares.*

'You always were sharp, Scott.'

'I've been called worse.'

Again, the smile. The first time I'd seen it was when she was a patrol officer with the Arrow Lake PD. It was to be her last year on patrol, as the Tom Morgan case had thrust her into the limelight. The Chief had seen the potential and had given her a promotion.

'I'd like you to come back with me,' she said.

'I went back once. It didn't do any good.' *I didn't find Jessie.*

. 'That was three years ago. I was a junior detective, promoted less than a year. This is different.' She reached a hand out and tapped the folder on the table with a perfectly manicured fingernail. Short but could still be stuck into an eyeball, if the fight turned into life-or-death. 'Back then, we didn't have any of the missing victims back.'

'And you want me to help you find the others.' I looked from her finger back to her eyes.

'I want your help more than anything. I caught this case and they're letting me run with it. I'm not too proud to call in outside help. And you're the only one who would be willing.'

'You make me sound like I'm part of a comedy trio; where's Ready and Able?'

The smile again. The one that had broken many hearts, I was sure.

'Would you be willing to come back with me, Scott? We couldn't pay a lot because our budget is tight, but I'm sure the Chief would put it to the board.'

I looked at her before answering. Would I be able to do that again, to go back to the town where I knew my partner had last been seen? Where I knew she was buried somewhere?

'This is going to sound stupid, but Atticus would be beside himself if I left him. I have a housekeeper, but I'm his dad.' I was making an excuse and it sounded like it.

'You can bring him with you. You can stay at my place. That would save money on a hotel. I haven't had a dog in my house since I lived with my folks. If you want to. I mean, no shenanigans obviously. On my part!' Her face started to go red. She put a hand up to her eyes and shook her head. 'Jesus.'

I knew then that I couldn't refuse her. 'I know what you meant. I'll come with you. I don't even need a consultancy fee. When do you want me there?' But I knew the answer when I looked in her eyes. 'I'll have to go home and get changed. And get Atticus's stuff together. He likes road trips.'

'We don't have to rush.'

I smiled at her. 'It'll be good to see Chief Walker again, I have to say.'

She looked down before answering. 'I'm afraid you won't be able to.'

'Why not?'

'He died six months ago. Hit and run.'

I sat shocked for a few seconds. 'Did you get anybody for it?'

Her look said it all.

TWO

I had been born in St Luke's Hospital down the road
from the college and had lived here in Newburgh until
I joined the FBI. It was an old city, and it got a bad rap
in the press, but there were pleasant areas too. I lived
on the fringe of the Historic District, with homes that
would have brought in a million dollars in other areas
of the country.

My house was a small detached, five minutes' walk
from the college, on Powell. Atticus greeted Dani like
she was his mom. Maria was my live-in housekeeper.
She had a little apartment downstairs in the basement
level, which suited her fine. Sure, I could have left
Atticus with her, but he wouldn't have eaten if I'd left
him behind. It was a thing with German Shepherds –
they got stressed if you went to the bathroom and
didn't tell them where you were going. I thought it was

unfair to leave him with Maria, so I explained where I was going, confident that at her age, she was past having parties in the house. Then she asked me if I would mind if she visited family and stayed with them for a few days?

I told her this was fine. She said she didn't need paying while she was away, but I told her paid vacation was okay. She smiled, said something in Spanish and gave me a big hug.

'You like Newburgh, huh?' Dani asked as I put my stuff and my dog in the back of her car. It was a two-year-old Chevy Tahoe. She had wanted a Jeep Wrangler, but her dad had wanted her to get a bigger car. I was grateful she hadn't brought one of the department's Ford Explorers with the hard, plastic prisoner seats in the back.

'I do,' I said to her as we pulled out of my shared driveway at the back of the house. It ran behind three houses and it meant we split the cost of any repairs. Maria waved us off like she was my mother. I promised her I'd call her, eat properly, and not stay up too late.

'I've been here before,' she said. 'To the city.'

I was surprised by this. She'd never told me about that, when I had worked with her before. 'Really?'

'I had a friend on the force who lived up here. He had a boat and we would go on it in the summer, from the Newburgh landing.'

'I always wanted a boat. I never got around to buying one. I should put it on my bucket list.'

'My dad has one. He bought it when he retired. If you ask him nicely, maybe he'll take you out on it.'

'Take me out and throw me overboard when he finds out I'm staying at your place.'

She laughed. 'He's not that bad.'

'I've met him, remember.'

'He just looks big and mean.'

'Some women buy a Rottweiler for protection. You don't need to.'

She smiled. I would probably be that protective if I had a daughter.

We took North Street to 9W and connected with I84.

'How does he like retirement?'

She shook her head. 'He was the county's Medical Examiner. Always on the go. It was bad enough when my mom retired, but now he's retired, he struggles to find things to do. My mom amuses herself, but Dad finds it hard switching off.'

'I can imagine how retirement can affect people who have worked all their lives.'

She merged with the traffic and I warned her about the New York State Troopers who sat at a spot around the corner. She kept the speed down as a tractor-trailer went by in a blur in the outside lane.

'You have anybody special in your life?' I asked her, then immediately regretted it.

'No. Have you?'

'No. I didn't mean that to sound like some cheesy pick-up line. I was just making sure nobody would object to me and the dog staying at your place. Apart from your dad.'

She smiled back. 'There's hardly an abundance of eligible bachelors in Arrow Lake. Unless you count old farmer Jack, but he must get up at four every morning and I need my sleep at the weekend.'

'I hear you. I don't miss the early rises.'

She pulled out into the passing lane and put her foot down. The V8 pulled us forward with ease. We connected with I87 at the interchange, which had the usual amount of afternoon traffic on it. Light but getting busier. The big red machine was comfortable, the air conditioning chilly as the sun dished out its relentless punishment.

I had worked closely with the detectives in Arrow Lake, along with my colleagues from the Behavioral Analysis Unit, BAU – 4. The detectives were a good bunch, but they didn't have the experience of detectives from a big city. That's where Dani came into her own; she had been an NYPD patrol officer for five years before going home to Arrow Lake.

'You have any pets?' I asked Dani.

Atticus poked his head up from the trunk area of the SUV before settling back down again.

She shook her head. 'My dog passed away. Max. We rescued him from a shelter in Queens where we lived.'

I looked out the windscreen, wanting to ask who the other half of *we* was, but figured it wasn't my business. Besides, she'd just told me that she didn't have anybody special in her life.

'How long have you been divorced?' I asked.

She gave a wry smile and glanced quickly at me before putting her eyes back on the road. 'Who said I was married? You figured that because I said *we*?'

'No. You moved back to the small town where you were brought up. It's what some folks do when they have a traumatic event in their life. Running back home. It's not a bad thing,' I added quickly, in case she took offence. Her smile said she hadn't. 'You're a good-looking woman, smart, intelligent so it figures you had somebody special in your life at one time.'

'Why not just a boyfriend? Why a husband?'

'Because you subconsciously rub the inside of your wedding finger with your thumb, as if you're still wearing a ring and you're trying to turn it.'

'You're some profiler, Scott, but you can only work out so much.' She smiled at me.

Atticus chuffed in the back as if he agreed with her.

I gripped the buff folder that was sitting in my lap. Dani and I had gotten to know each other a little better, three years ago, but she had kept her private life to herself, except to tell me there was nobody special in her life at the time.

I settled back and opened the folder. Looked at the gruesome sight of what had once been a healthy human being, reduced to nothing but a memory by a man who had fooled us all. And now she had been found by somebody else and discarded like a piece of trash.

Except this person was cleverer than that. She hadn't been discarded but put on center stage.

I read the notes. And found my mind drifting to Jessie Kent. My partner and one of the best profilers on the BAU team. The term *profiler* didn't officially exist in the FBI and Jessie wasn't shy in reminding people of that fact.

I put the notes away, closed the file and slipped it back into my messenger bag. I closed my eyes and let the cold air from the vents wash over my face.

The drive would take three hours and we'd only been on the road for half an hour. I closed my eyes and started to think of four years ago.

———

'Scott, wake up!' Special Agent Jessie Kent stood at the side of my bed and shook me awake. The hotel room was small and the bed hard so I wasn't getting a good night's sleep. I'd been reading a file but instead of sitting at the small desk, I'd laid on the bed, which was a mistake. I'd switched off the air con and the hot air had rapidly taken over the room. I'd dozed off.

'I was just resting my eyes,' I said, yawning.

'I don't know where you learned to snore like that while you're awake, but you've got it down to a fine art.'

'I swear we were married in another life, and now you've come back to nag me all over again.'

'Just looking after you. Time for dinner.'

I looked over at the open door.

'Yes,' Jessie said to me, 'the door wasn't locked. I could have been our killer.'

I looked at her for a moment. Shrugged. 'I've got nothing,' I said, a viable excuse refusing to come to my aid.

The hotel was part of a chain, nondescript rooms the same the world over. Close your eyes and you could pretend you were in Paris, or England. The food was all American though.

'I've been thinking about our guy,' Jessie said, when we had ordered some dinner. She was a year younger *than me but she had so much enthusiasm for the job, that I could see her sitting in the big chair in Washington one day.*

'Tell me,' I said, drinking some of my soda.

'We talked about how we thought he was a local. He knows the area like the back of his hand. He blends right in. Nobody questions him when they see him walk by.'

'Agreed. I remember the team talking about it.'

'I got to thinking; who goes about town and nobody sees him? I mean, obviously they see him, but look right through him.'

I looked at her before answering. 'The mailman.'

'Postal carrier, Scott. They have women doing the job too.'

'But we agreed this is the work of a man. Hence, mailman.'

'Okay. Mailman, or garbage collector. Or any utility worker. The cable guy, sanitation worker. They are all there, working away, nobody paying attention to them.'

'Good. We can collect names and run them through the database. See where they were at the times when the women were taken.'

'And we can check if any of them were near where the women lived.'

'We can get onto that tomorrow. City Hall will be closed now. Cable company will be closed. We'll get *onto it first thing in the morning, but we can talk to the rest of the team later tonight.'*

Jessie was always enthusiastic. She was the only agent I knew who couldn't switch off. She'd never been married and the thought of getting into a long-term relationship wasn't at the top of her to-do list.

After dinner, Jessie wanted to do some work on her laptop. I wanted to take a drive along North Shore Drive, on the edge of the lake. I wanted to go to the park where one of the women had been seen last, jogging. Jessie told me she was going to meet somebody, who might have some information.

Ashbury Park. Right down by the river.

'Get an early night,' Jessie said to me in the lobby. 'We have an early start.'

'I'll be fine. I'll just drink plenty of coffee.'

'You'll never learn, will you?' she said and smiled at me as the lift doors closed.

It was the last time I ever saw her.

THREE

'I saw the dead girl,' Bill Fox said, sitting down at his daughter's kitchen table. Atticus had sniffed him out, deeming him to be friend, rather than foe. Much to Bill's relief.

'Did Lou know what her cause of death could have been?' Dani asked. *Lou Fazio.* The new county Medical Examiner, the man who'd taken over from Bill four years ago.

Bill slid the folder over so it sat in the middle. We were sitting drinking coffee, and the folder was between us, like a deck of cards. The perils of having a little round table in the kitchen. Her dining room had been made into an office, she said.

I could see Dani wanted to open it but I guessed she felt that I should look at it first. I slid it across to her.

'The poor girl was in a pretty bad way before she was dumped,' Bill said, drinking coffee. Dani poured over the preliminary report and the photos of the corpse as she lay on the steel table in the autopsy suite.

'How have things been with you since we last met?' Bill said.

I'd come back to town a year after we left, having made no headway in finding Jessie or the other four women. Seven victims in total, including Jessie, only two of them found. Lying in open, shallow graves. *Come and find me!* That had been the message he had been sending, and we did, but not before he did massive damage to so many lives.

'I have my private investigator's license, but I don't do much investigating these days. I'm also a lecturer at a local college,' I said. 'Nothing exciting but it pays the bills. I teach criminology.'

'There's no better teacher than a former FBI agent, I guess.'

'Some might argue that one.' I drank more of the coffee as Bill sat and looked at me for a moment, like a father might look at a boy who's going to take his daughter to the prom. He had what I assumed was a *You touch my daughter, I'll kill you* look about him.

'You could have stayed over at our place,' he said. 'We have plenty of room now it's just the two of us.'

'Dad!' Dani looked up from the folder. 'I told Scott

he could stay here, so it wouldn't cost a hotel room. We know him. *I* trust him.' She stared him in the eye. 'I'm not fifteen.'

'He's only looking out for you, Dani,' I said to her. Then looked at Bill. 'But if it makes you uncomfortable for me to stay with your daughter, sir, I can find another place. I don't want to upset anybody.'

'Christ, Dad, I'm a cop. He was an FBI agent. It's hardly going to be *Animal House*.'

'I'm just saying,' Bill said, at least having the decency to blush. I imagined that didn't happen very often. 'After what that moron did to you.'

'Again. Maybe we could focus on the matter at hand?' She looked at me. 'He means my ex-husband.'

Bill sighed and drank more coffee. 'Don't pay any heed to me, son. I trust you. Any man who has a German Shepherd is alright in my book.'

I looked at the list of names of *The Gravedigger's* victims. I hated thinking of him by that name. I corrected myself; the victims of Detective Tom Morgan, of the Arrow Lake Police Department.

Six women, all taken within a three-month period, in the summer, four years earlier. Then he took my partner.

In my line of work, hunting down men and women who would do things to other human beings that most people couldn't comprehend, you get to be a little bit jaded. Look at people slightly differently than other people would.

I had looked Tom Morgan in the eye and I didn't see the monster inside. None of us had. But there had been a monster there all the time.

'You okay, Scott?' Dani asked.

'I was just thinking about Jessie,' I said.

Bill looked at me. 'It must be hard for you, son. She was a great woman. I was gutted when he took her.'

'Me too, Bill. It's hard right enough, but I'm here to find her, if I can. Find whoever's found the body of that girl.'

The folder that I had been reading in the car was on the table. I pulled it towards me and opened it up. Took out the list of names that was inside.

Ellen Wood, age 26

Angela Kerr, age 33

Patti Ross, age 25

Brittany Lowe, age 21

Alice Neil, age 24

Donna Taylor, age 27

Jessie Kent, age 30

'I'd like to go to the morgue tomorrow,' I said to Dani.

'I'll call ahead first thing in the morning.'

'Well, I'm going home for dinner. You're both welcome to join us,' Bill said, standing up from the table.

Dani looked at her father and for the first time, I could see the tiredness in her eyes. 'Thanks, Dad. Maybe a rain check?'

He laughed. 'Anytime. Your mother always makes too much anyway.'

He petted Atticus before he left. The dog stood at the front door as if he thought Bill was going to come back in. Then he turned and went into the corner where I'd laid his blanket.

'I'll cook something for us,' Dani said, rubbing her eyes. It was well past six. Atticus had already eaten, so he was good.

'How about we find some place that's pet friendly and we can eat out?' I said.

'There's a pizza place just off Main Street that allows dogs to sit outside on their patio. The pizza is great.'

'Let's go.'

We drove down from her house, the summer sun still high but slipping down closer to the trees that lined the far side of Arrow Lake. The lake was huge, with dozens of houses surrounding it.

'It's still as busy as I remember it,' I said, taking the dog over to a grass verge that lined the parking lot. I

24

had my backpack on, with water for Atticus. He would normally walk by my side but in a strange place, I preferred him to be on a leash.

'It's just as busy in the winter months when we get hit with the snow. From the beginning of December through to mid-March, Arrow Lake becomes a ski resort.'

Right now, it was a place to get away to, for water skiing, hiking, boating. You could rent a mountain bike or an ATV. Me, I preferred to take Atticus for a walk. There were plenty of rail trails near Newburgh.

'I'll order if you want to sit at a table with Atticus,' I said to Dani. It was busy but not a lot of people wanted to sit out in the hot air, preferring to sit in the comfort of the air con.

'Okay. Pepperoni slice, please. And a seltzer.'

Atticus wanted to drink from the bowl the owner kept out for dogs, but I wanted him to have the cold stuff. I took one of the dog biscuits for him though.

The server said she would bring our food out so I joined Dani, bringing our bottles of soda. The patio overlooked the roadway below that skirted the lake. People were enjoying the last of the sun, strolling with their families.

I took a sip of the Coke. 'Did you see her?' I asked Dani.

'Red shirt, dark blue shorts, sunglasses with a Yankees cap?'

'That's her. She's been watching us since we parked the car. Do you recognize her?'

She laughed, in case the girl was watching what we were saying from her spot across the road. She was sitting at a pavement café, drinking from a bottle of soda. She had a bag that she had put on another chair.

'No. She could be anybody though.'

'She got out of a car that had been driving behind us, then she hovered around while I took Atticus over for a pee.' The dog perked his ears up at the mention of his name. I rubbed his ear and he lay back down.

'After our pizza, we'll see if she's still around.'

The young girl came out with our food and we tucked in. I was hungrier than I thought I'd be. 'Your dad hasn't changed much,' I said.

'In attitude or physical appearance?'

I grinned. 'Both, I guess.'

'He's always been over protective.' She wiped her face and looked at me. 'He didn't say anything when I moved down to New York, but my mum said it broke his heart to see his little girl leave him.'

'I think I would feel the same way if I had a daughter.'

'It was hard for him to see me go, especially when I was joining the NYPD.'

'How did he take it when you split up with your husband? If that's not too personal.'

'He was gutted. He'd relaxed knowing that I had somebody in my life down there, looking after me.'

'Divorce is always tough.'

'You've never been married, have you?'

'Once. We were young and foolish. But she decided that Hollywood was for her. The acting bug got her, and she tried to get me to go to LA with her, get a transfer to a field office, but I had my heart set on the BAU. So, she waved adios and I never heard from her again. For a while, anyway.'

'Did she ever make it in the movies?'

'No, but she did get a part on a soap, *Loves and Lives*.'

Dani's eyes widened. 'No way! I watch that all the time. What's her name?'

'Lucy Diamond.'

'Jesus, no. *Claire Deveraux?*'

'Yep. That's her.'

'Have you ever seen her again?'

'A few times. When she's been over here on the East Coast, just to say hi. Her and her husband.'

'Wow. I know somebody who knows Lucy Diamond.'

'You sound like an awe-struck teenager,' I said, laughing. I nonchalantly looked across the road. The girl was still there and turned her head away when I looked over.

'I do, don't I?' She laughed, and I felt comfortable being in her company. My guts had felt twisted all the way up here on the drive, and I knew I was going to be on edge like I had drunk a gallon of coffee every day, but I had a feeling Dani would be there to steady me.

We ate in silence for a few minutes, a sudden feeling of guilt sweeping over me. Here I was, laughing and having dinner with a beautiful woman, while Jessie was lying dead somewhere.

Dani reached over and put a hand on mine. 'It's okay, Scott. I was there, a long time ago. It's life. It's how we deal with things and learn to move on. You can laugh and smile, it doesn't take away what you felt for Jessie.'

Christ, it was like she had read my mind. 'I know. I find it hard sometimes. I saw a therapist for a while. She helped me put myself on the straight and narrow, but it hurts now and then. Knowing two of us travelled up here together, and only one of us left. Out of the whole team, three got to go home.'

She took her hand away gently. Looked at me. 'I know how you feel.'

'Do you?' I said, not wanting to say any more. People always said they knew how you felt, but they didn't have a clue.

'Yes,' she said quietly. If she hadn't taken her sunglasses off and laid them on the table, I wouldn't have seen the tears in her eyes.

I didn't know what else to say to her, so I pulled off a piece of my pizza crust and fed it to Atticus, who was acting like he hadn't seen food in days. We were comfortable in the shade of the umbrella.

'What was it like growing up here?' I asked her.

'Busier than you would think,' she said, her smile back in place.

'What made you go to work for the NYPD?' I realized that although I'd worked with her before, there was very little I knew about Dani Fox.

'I wanted to see a bit of life. Some people live in Arrow Lake all their lives, but I wanted to see the big city lights. Joining the force down there gave me that chance.'

'It certainly is a big difference. Did you like it?' I turned my head slightly, looking with my peripheral vision. The woman was still across the road, watching us, pretending not to watch us.

'I need to get something from the car,' I said, getting up. Atticus got up, because his dad was moving. Dani kept a hold of him while I crossed the road, not looking in the direction of the woman, then walked into the parking lot.

The café where the woman was sitting bordered

the entrance to the parking lot. She didn't see me come back round. I moved quickly, pulling out a chair and sitting down.

'You don't mind if I join you, do you?'

Before she could speak, Dani was across with Atticus, standing next to her.

The woman was about to say something but then she deflated.

'I'm Detective Fox of the Arrow Lake PD,' Dani said, showing her badge.

'I know who you are,' she said.

'We don't know who *you* are,' Dani said. Atticus watched the young woman, tail not wagging yet, picking up his signals from us.

The young woman looked to be around mid-twenties or so. She took off her Yankees baseball cap and threw it on the table. 'I'm Cathy Kerr, Angela Kerr's cousin.' She rummaged about in her pocketbook and came out with a driver's license. Dani took it and looked at it before handing it back.

'Why were you following us?' I asked. Atticus started swinging his tail, sensing no threat. He nudged Cathy's arm and she petted him.

She looked at me as Dani sat down on another seat. 'I heard about you finding a body not too far from the lake. I wondered if it was connected to Angela's murder. I had to come over here.' She looked at Dani. 'I followed you home from the station last night. Sorry. I wanted to knock on your door, but I didn't have it in me. I didn't see you today, but I hung around your neighborhood. Then I saw you pull up with this man.'

'My name's Scott Marshall. I'm ex-FBI.'

'I remember you from the last time, I couldn't remember your name. I recognized you though.'

'What did you hope to achieve by following us?' Dani asked.

Tears started rolling down the girl's face. 'I'm scared. This girl being found, well, it brought it all back to me.' She looked at Dani. 'Is it Angela?'

'It's too soon to tell.'

'Who would do such a thing?' she asked me. I didn't have the correct answer but felt she needed something.

'Somebody dangerous.'

'It's not kids having a lark about?' She looked me in the eyes, searching for hope and finding none.

'No.' There wasn't anything else I could add to soften the blow.

'Do you live here?' Dani asked.

'I used to. I moved away to Spring Lake not far from here. I couldn't live in town anymore. I was a nurse over at the hospital with Angela. We were more like sisters. It was different when she was gone.'

'Are you still a nurse?'

'Yes. The little hospital over there isn't as exciting, but it's away from here.'

'Have you seen any strangers lurking about?' I asked her.

'No.'

'Just be aware of your surroundings when you're out and about,' I said.

'Get somebody to walk you to your car when you finish work,' Dani said. 'Women everywhere should take precautions.'

'I will.' She stood up and grabbed her bag. 'Thanks for listening to me.'

I gave her a business card with my cell number on it. 'Call me if you need us. Or call the station. Either way.'

She walked away into the parking lot.

'Do you think she's genuine?' Dani asked me.

'I do. Or else she's a perfect liar. I've had both sitting across from me in an interrogation room, but I think she's genuine.'

We walked back to the car, Atticus sniffing around, on the scent of another dog.

In the house, I went through to the kitchen to switch on the coffee pot when I saw the piece of paper lying on the floor, having been slid under the back door.

I took out a pair of gloves out of habit and slipped them on. Read the writing on the paper. The warning was simple:

Go home, Scott.

FOUR

Dani's spare room was furnished like a spare room should be: bed, dresser, and a chair. The bed was a double size, which meant I got six inches of mattress to lie on, while Atticus made himself at home, stretched diagonally. It was a good arrangement in winter, not so much in summer.

I slept fitfully, and Atticus did his usual drumming on my legs, his nightly dream-fueled tattoo.

Go home, Scott.

We'd talked about the note for over an hour. I had taken Atticus out to scout about round the house and he had picked up some kind of scent, which could have been our mystery note writer or it could just as easily have been a raccoon.

Dani's house wasn't too isolated, the next-door house being within shouting distance. The back yard stretched into the woods, which ran uphill and led to the lake. Not *the* lake, but a big enough lake to take a boat out on, but not so big it could be mistaken for Arrow Lake. It was connected to the big lake itself, and the topography could lend camouflage to somebody who wanted to slip a note under the bottom of a back door and leave again unnoticed.

After my shower, I went downstairs and started cooking breakfast.

'I'd like you to meet the new chief today,' Dani said, as I flipped the eggs and bacon. Atticus had been out, had chowed down on his breakfast, and was expecting a slice of bacon while we waited on Bill. He'd called when Dani was in the shower and offered to take the dog for the day. I'd said okay, as he would have had to be left in the car with the air con blasting otherwise.

'What's she like?'

'Arrogant. Knows better than everybody else.'

I'd met her sort before, trying to prove herself in a man's world, but the prejudices she encountered were all in her mind. 'How does she feel about me coming here?' I slipped the bacon and eggs onto a plate. It was just for me. Dani ate oatmeal and had a glass of OJ.

'She was very nonchalant about it. Like we could deal with this ourselves, but if you wanted to come along for the ride, then that was okay.'

We ate breakfast, Atticus having a slice of bacon and sitting by my side, wanting more but being sorely disappointed. Dani packed a small sports bag with two bottles and two energy bars.

'I'll fill them later,' she said, not expounding on where she would fill them. I hoped it wasn't going to be the lake.

After Bill took Atticus away in his truck, we headed over to the station, which was in the middle of town.

It was a two-story building on the corner of Main Street and Lake Drive. Several cruisers were parked round the back of the building when Dani pulled in.

Inside, Chief Nikki Hunter was waiting for us. 'Take a seat, Agent Marshall.'

'It's just *Scott* these days,' I said to her.

She shrugged. There was no smile, no handshake. I could tell from the red creeping onto Dani's cheeks that there had been a bigger issue with me coming here than she had let on.

'You've had a chance to read the report on the body we found, I take it,' she said.

'I have.' We sat down, Dani and I next to each other, facing the Chief. I guessed she was in her thirties, a divorcee. Lines were starting to form round her eyes, and I was thinking that wasn't from working here for the last six months. She was a transplant from somewhere else.

'First impressions?'

I held her eye contact for a second. Out the window at her back, I could see a Starbucks directly across the road. People coming and going with cold drinks. People sitting outside at pavement tables. There were a lot of places in this town that encouraged people to sit outside of their establishments.

'First impressions, we have a twisted individual on our hands. He stumbled across either one or all the previous victims.'

'Any idea why somebody would go to such lengths to display one?'

'We won't know exactly why they did this until we find them. Sometimes we can explain why they do things, then there are those people who defy explanation. Maybe it's somebody's idea of a joke.'

'Sick joke, if you ask me.'

'I agree. But whoever he is, he wants attention. And he's getting it.'

She sat back in her chair and looked at me. 'Detective Fox wanted to bring you on board because you were on the case four years ago. And because your partner was abducted. I was reluctant to bring you here, as I thought you wouldn't be able to focus. I want you to prove me wrong.'

And there we had it. Addressing the elephant in the room. I sat and looked at her, not saying anything, before she continued.

'Tom Morgan's family left town a little while after his death. *Run out of town* they would have called it years ago. They were hounded, paint was sprayed on his wife's front door, his son was bullied in high school. His daughter was ridiculed in elementary. What the people in this town did was deplorable.'

I studied her face for a moment. 'Haven't you only been in this job six months?'

'Yes. Why?'

'How do you know they were treated like that?'

'My father was the chief before me. I was a lieutenant in Rochester. I applied for this job when my dad died.'

'I worked with your father when I was here with my team. I was sorry to hear of his passing.'

She nodded her head slightly, as if the memory of Chief Walker had taken her back to another time and place.

'I'm happy for you to shadow Detective Fox but let me tell you this to your face; if you step out of line once, you'll be asked to leave. Do I make myself clear?'

Run out of town I thought again. 'Crystal,' I said, smiling. It was a smile I thought conveyed pity rather than humor.

Dani stood up and looked at the Chief. 'We'll keep you in the loop.'

I expected a sarcastic remark fired from the hip in return, but Nikki Hunter was a woman still hurting, and I could see in her eyes that she wanted to make friends in this town but they were having none of it.

'Nice meeting you, Chief,' I said, holding my hand out. She reached over and shook it, her grip strong and confident.

She made eye contact and nodded. I thought she was trying to reach for some words at that point but couldn't voice them. She had to maintain a strong exterior, and her voice would have given the game away.

Dani and I left the building without her exchanging any pleasantries with the other detectives in the squad.

'Don't you usually go to your desk in the morning?' I asked her.

'Yes. But I'm eager to get on. Let's hit the Starbucks across the road before we head over to the hospital. They're expecting us. I think I need to add more rocket fuel to my system.'

'I'm not going to argue with that.' I didn't say that I really wanted to argue with her reasoning, that she was eager to get across to the mortuary. What she meant was, she didn't want the other detectives meeting me, but I knew I would have to one day soon. The others knew who I was. Maybe that was the reason. Mister big-shot FBI waltzes in and solves the case, one hand behind his back, blindfolded, and all before lunch. Done and dusted.

'My dad won't mind if you want to call and see if Atticus is doing okay,' Dani said, getting in behind the wheel of her car.

'I'm sure he'll be fine. But if you want to call later and check to see if my dog's eaten the UPS guy, feel free.' I smiled at her and she drove across the road. We picked up two coffees. Just plain coffee for me and something that I wouldn't remember the name of in a million years for Dani. Coffee is coffee. It made me feel old just thinking that but I didn't want to blow a month's salary adding toppings to my morning brew.

I picked up the file from the passenger footwell and flipped through it again, between sips.

'What were your initial thoughts when you learned of another woman being discovered?' I asked her.

She navigated the Tahoe like a race car driver.

'I couldn't believe it, Scott. It was like living this nightmare all over again.' She looked over at me. 'I thought of you again.'

I grabbed my coffee out of the cup holder. As we left town, the ski jump was on our left, sitting unused while it waited for the winter snow. My mind thought back to three years ago, on the anniversary of the killings. To a lonely night in the lakeside cabin that had once belonged to her grandfather. To the log fire that spat sparks out into a darkened living room and to a glass of wine.

Dani and I spent the night together, two lonely people, finding solace in the company of another lonely, human being. We didn't regret it in the morning. She had held onto me and told me so, and I assured her that was the case for me. Just two lonely people, not lonely for one night.

'Yes, I do,' she said, smiling at me.

'Yes, you do what?' I asked her, wondering if I'd blurted out asking her to marry me.

'Still have my grandfather's cabin, but not for much longer. Atticus would love it there. You remember the dock out back where we had the old boat tied up?'

'I do,' I replied, like she'd just tricked me into repeating her words in front of the minister.

'My dad spent two summers remodeling it. And we got a new boat. Just something my dad can go out fishing on. But unfortunately, my folks sold the cabin. All the cabins were bought by Magnus Porter. He's going to build huge houses on each lot and make a fortune.'

What was I supposed to say then? *Great! Let's go back up there again one night.* 'Sounds good,' I said, and I felt the answer came out of my subconscious, something from the mental handbook of how to interrogate prisoners.

'We should have a barbeque up there one night. Get the family round. Before they have to hand it over, which is going to happen very soon.'

'I'm sure your dad's a genius on the grill.'

'Don't tell him that. It'll go straight to his head.'

'Okay. I'll tell him he's not as good as me.'

'Oh God, and start World War III?' She laughed.

We made some more small talk until we reached the hospital, which seemed a big affair for a small town, until I remembered that it served a wide area.

The morgue entrance was round the back. The medical examiner's van was parked outside roller doors that were shut.

Dani finished her coffee. I took mine with me. I left the folder in the car.

Lou Fazio was a man in his early forties, I guessed. That's where the resemblance ended; he was built like a football player, with a shaved head and a goatee beard, as if somebody had turned his head upside down. He wore round-framed glasses and had an easy smile. He stood a good few inches taller than my six two.

'I've heard a lot about you,' he said. We shook hands.

'The big, bad sheriff rides into town. I feel like Wyatt Earp.'

'I bet you don't know his two middle names,' Fazio said.

'Berry Stapp,' Dani answered.

'That's not fair. I was asking him.'

'I watched the movie *Tombstone* then googled the man,' Dani said.

'Googling is cheating.'

I looked at Dani with raised eyebrows.

'What? I like westerns.'

'Add that to the list of things I didn't know about Detective Dani Fox,' I said, thinking she was yanking my chain.

'Do you have a result on the ID?' Dani asked as we headed through to the autopsy suite.

'I do indeed. But you're not going to like it.' He had a lazy eye that went off to one side and I kept focusing on it. 'It was why we were having difficulty identifying her.'

I had a feeling in the pit of my stomach when he said that. Not one I got often. Profiling all sorts of killers gave us a sort of immunity to feeling sick, but Jessie's smile shot into my mind. Her kind face, her razor-sharp wit, and her damned fine profiling skills.

The stainless-steel tables were gleaming, showing no signs of having had a rotting corpse on them. Other staff members bustled about, one coming in for a moment before leaving just as quickly.

We entered a room off the autopsy room and I remembered this is where the human fridges were located. The penultimate resting place for some people.

Fazio gripped the handle on one of the square, steel doors and opened it. The table glided out with the body on it, like it was some kind of magic show he was rehearsing.

It was at hip height, and I wondered if he had chosen this one especially for our impending visit.

He gripped the top of the sheet and looked at us both before proceeding. Like he was about to say, *Ladies and Gentlemen, a big hand for Fazio the Magnificent!*

We both nodded and he gently pulled the sheet up. No puff of smoke, no sleight of hand.

The girl was in a bad way. In a way that might have made the uninitiated throw up. Hair was still on the skull, and there were traces of muscle and skin, but being in the ground had taken its toll on this poor woman.

'Cause of death?' Dani asked.

'Strangulation.'

We were skirting round the next question, circling

the wagons around the answer we wanted to surrender but knew might come out fighting.

'Who is she, Lou?' I asked, firing the first arrow.

He put the sheet back, giving a little bit of dignity to a woman who had lost all of it when she died at the hands of another. I wasn't expecting him to answer, but he surprised me.

'Nicky Hunter called when you were on the way over. They got a hit. Her name is Sofia Martinez. Age twenty-seven. She went missing over four years ago.'

'Her name isn't on our list,' I said, feeling my mouth going dry. He'd thrown us a curve ball and I got the feeling I couldn't duck in time.

'That's correct. Sofia came from the Bronx. She went to a nightclub in Manhattan with a friend and was last seen getting in a car with a man. She was reported missing later that day by her sister. They were supposed to go shopping for wedding dresses for her sister, but Sofia didn't turn up.'

'Surely somebody saw who she left with?' I said. 'Witnesses.'

'Of course they did. The ones who came forward. And depending which one you believed, he was either five foot five or six foot seven. He had dark hair or blond hair. He had longish curly hair. One said he had a tattoo on the inside of one arm, like an army badge or something. He wore glasses. They left in a nondescript sports car.'

'Who was she there with?' Dani asked.

'A friend of hers, who went home with another man. She didn't see who Sofia was dancing with. You know the scene: low lights, drink flowing. Everybody spilling out at the same time, looking for taxis. Getting into cars.'

'What time of year was it?' I asked.

'Spring. It was raining hard when they got out, according to one witness.'

'Makes sense why they didn't want to hang around,' Dani said.

I drank more of my now lukewarm coffee then walked over to a small sink at the edge of the room and poured the remains out and dumped the cup.

Turned to face the other two.

'How would you profile this?' Fazio asked, throwing down the gauntlet.

'He's a very clever man. Sofia was taken before the others, so maybe she was intended to be the first to be put on display. Tom Morgan was very confident, and smart. He not only killed her but brought her up here and buried her.'

'Maybe the media pressure,' Dani said. 'After all, this was a girl from the Bronx, not some small town.

Maybe he figured that was a fast track to getting caught, so he decided to bury her.'

'He's certainly not shy. He met her in a nightclub full of people, offered her a ride in his car, again in front of people, then took her to his hometown.'

'He was taking a risk driving her all the way here,' Fazio said.

'What risk? He hadn't forced her into the car. Maybe he told her he was rich, and would she like to go upstate with him? If he got pulled over, it was all innocent. Or, he might have stopped somewhere and killed her, then put her in the trunk and driven her here. If he got pulled over, he was a cop remember, he could talk his way out of it. Or shoot the officer who had pulled him over. It was a rush for him.'

'I would go for him killing her well before he got here,' Dani said.

'I agree.'

'Why?' Fazio said.

'She was going to go shopping for wedding dresses the next day. Not something I think she would give up to travel upstate with a stranger.'

'He would likely tell her he lived close by,' I said, 'that way she wouldn't mind getting in the car. Not far from home.'

'It was still a risk for him to come all this way and hide her,' Fazio said.

'He knew the area very well. People who can bury somebody like he did would know the most likely spots to put her. Whoever found her and decided to play games, knows this place like the back of his hand.' I looked at Dani and the doctor. 'There's something else we need to add into the equation.'

'What's that?' Dani said.

'Sofia was a victim we never knew about. There could be others. Who knows how long Tom Morgan was killing?'

FIVE

'I'm going to get in touch with my ex,' Dani said. 'His precinct is in Mid Town. He can check up for me. Give us some more details on the disappearance. They can get their colleagues in the Bronx to give the death notice. Then we can check to see if Morgan was on call or something that Saturday night. See if anybody knew of his whereabouts.'

'Then there's going to be an even bigger circus in town. *Missing woman from the Bronx found dead in an upstate town where serial killer struck.* I can imagine the headline now,' Fazio said.

'Good idea. Meantime, I'd like to visit the site where Sofia was put.'

'I'll swing over there now. It's up in the hills, near the north end of the lake.'

We left the morgue and headed back into town.

Thankfully, Dani had filled the water bottles from the drinking fountain in the hospital.

She pressed the call button on her steering wheel and I heard a phone ringing through the speakers. 'I thought you might want to check in on your little boy.'

'Hello?' the voice said on the other end.

'Hey, Dad. How's Atticus? You're on speaker in my car.'

'Hey, you two. Atticus said he wants to come up here and live permanently, he likes it so much.'

'I think Scott might have something to say about that.'

Bill laughed. 'He's having the time of his life, running about in one of the fenced off areas. Or was, I should say. He's having a nap now. Like me and your mother should be doing.'

'You're not that old.'

'Sometimes my old bones tell me otherwise. But tell me how you got on with young Lou.'

'Get this; the girl was reported missing four years ago. From the Bronx.'

'Whoa. Back the truck up a bit. She doesn't come from around here?'

'Nope. She accepted a lift from a stranger and was never heard from again. Died of strangulation.'

'What do you know? That would make sense.'

'Why does that make sense, Bill?' I asked.

'Tom Morgan was originally NYPD. He would know his way around there. It wouldn't be too much of a stretch to think he was down there, maybe visiting people he knew, then went to a club in Manhattan.'

I wanted to speak to her now. I wanted to talk to her about her husband, the man we knew as a serial killer.

'Thanks, Dad. We'll be round later to pick up the dog.'

'Don't rush. He's fine.'

She disconnected the call and drove on in silence for a little while. It was sunny outside, but the breeze made it feel colder than it looked. A few clouds slid across the sky but nothing that made us think the day was going to get worse.

Dani drove through some residential streets until we reached the other side of town and turned off the road into a parking lot. Ashbury Park. There were two lots, north and south. We went over to the north one, which was smaller. Trails started from both parking lots and connected so it was possible to start in the north and end up back at the south.

A few cars were parked in the gravel parking lot.

'Popular place,' I said as she pulled up next to an old Subaru Forester. An old, dark green model that looked like it would go on forever.

'Hikers, mostly. Some bring mountain bikes up here. Up at the top, there's a beautiful view of the lake.'

I got out and stretched. Swatted some bugs away. I made a mental note to get some spray at the pharmacy in town. Atticus had his flea and tick prevention up to date for the month, so he was good to go.

'Walk me through the informant's statement again, since we're here and this is where he said he started.'

I looked around. Several trails left the parking lot, with carved signs pointing the way. Each trail had a name. Maybe so the emergency dispatcher knew where to send help when one of the weekend warriors got himself into trouble.

I pulled on the police baseball cap that Dani had brought for me. I felt comfortable wearing it, just like I still felt comfortable wearing the Glock under my shirt. Some habits die hard.

'Atticus would like it here,' I said, as we started up the path called *Hiker's Ridge*.

'We should bring him up here one night.'

Anybody overhearing our conversation might have mistook us for a couple who lived here, instead of two law enforcement officers. It was only my second day here, but I was already picturing in my mind finding Jessie and then leaving town.

I wanted nothing more than to find her, but then I would be out of Dani Fox's life once more.

My mind was reaching into the future, full of *What if's.* Like finding Jessie and having to take her up north to Maine, to her family. I had spoken to them and although they didn't come out and say it, I knew they blamed me for her disappearance.

I was the one who was tasked to look after her, in their minds, although Jessie was a very competent FBI agent who was superb on the firing range.

People reacted in different ways when it came to grief, and Jessie's family hit out at me. I didn't blame them. Her sister had come down from Portland and we'd talked. I didn't mend her heart but helped her to understand. Most of all I told her how I would never give up hope of finding Jessie one day.

The trees created a canopy above us, giving us relief from the early afternoon sun. The path was crushed stone, rolled flat. It was meant to be easier on the feet of the hikers who came into town to spend money.

'These tracks used to be much harder to walk on,' Dani said as we crested the top of a hill. 'That's why they put the stones down. A visitor in hospital with a broken ankle can't be in town spending money.'

'That makes sense.' I felt a burn in my knee. Tom Morgan had kicked it sideways back on that day, and I'd fallen face down into the undergrowth. As the pain shot through my leg, it was overshadowed by being shot five times.

I could still see it now, clear as day; as I lay on the flattened grass and weeds, my face was turned to the left. I couldn't speak, but even if I could, I don't know what I could have said to stop Morgan from killing me.

I couldn't focus on his face. Instead, I was focused on the revolver he had been using. I saw it through the blood mingling with the tears, inches from my face. I focused on the barrel, at the small, dark tunnel where a high-speed train was going to come out in the shape of a bullet and switch my life off. The first bullet hit my head, ploughing a trench across my forehead, causing blood to run down my face. Six bullets in total. That's why he took the automatic out and pointed that at my face.

And he didn't pull the trigger.

I didn't hear the shouts of the others. They told me all about it later.

If some of the uniforms hadn't distracted Morgan, he would have pulled the trigger and I would have taken a bullet in the head.

The first officer shouted and fired at the same time, missing Morgan but causing him to use the last bullet to return fire. He missed but he had another gun and used it to fire off shots while he ran, putting distance between himself and me.

'Jesus, Scott, are you okay?' Dani said. Her hand was warm on my arm.

I looked at her, puzzled, then felt the river of sweat running down my neck and face.

'I'm fine,' I said, but I didn't want to take another step forward in case I fell face first onto the stone path.

I was shaking, my legs were shaking. My mouth had gone dry. Christ, was I ready for this?

Dani was taking a bottle out of the bag and handed it to me. As I drank, she took out an energy bar and unwrapped it, passing it over to me. I looked at it like I didn't know what to do with it.

'Are you diabetic?' she asked, standing up.

'Type two,' I said. 'But my doctor said it's border-line and if I work on my weight a bit more, it can be reversed.'

'Low blood sugar. Eat this.'

I took the bar and ate it, washing it down with some water. I didn't want to tell her the shakes were the result of a nightmare I'd had for the last four years. Not an every night, PTSD nightmare, but an event that I kept going over in my head, wishing for a different outcome, one where I overpowered Morgan and shot him dead.

I wanted to tell Dani all of this, but I smiled instead. 'Thanks.'

She smiled back, in a sad way, as if she had just helped an elderly person cross a busy street.

'Small and often,' she said.

'I know. I usually have a bowl of soup for lunch.'

'No bowls of soup up here,' she said, and I waited for her to follow it up with, *grandpa*, but she said nothing.

We walked round the corner as the path descended, the trees no longer affording us shade, but the view of the lake was spectacular from up here.

Or would have been if it wasn't for the new construction going on further along, on the south side. New condos and houses were being built on a clearing overlooking the lake, and I could practically see the dollar signs. Somebody was going to be making a lot of money from these homes.

'Wow. Who owns that lot?'

'Who do you think?' Dani said, her back still to me.

I thought she was going to say Donald Trump, but by her silence, I guessed it was the local millionaire in town.

'Magnus Porter.'

She turned and looked at me. 'Correct. Only he could get away with taking down a hillside and sticking up houses. Nobody else would get something like that past the planning board.'

The building site was a mix of houses that were

waiting the final touch and wooden skeletons under construction.

'They're going to add a clubhouse right down by the water,' she said, turning back.

I could see why. The lake was serene, the sunlight shimmering on the glasslike surface. I could imagine enjoying a beer on a deck overlooking the water.

'It's so peaceful here—' Dani said as the first shot rang out. The noise cracked through the still afternoon air and we both ducked instinctively as the bullet ricocheted off a tree.

We drew our weapons as we ran for cover behind a tree that was thick enough to hide both of us.

'Did you see where it came from?' Dani asked.

'The piece of bark that flew off moved in a southerly direction. He's up the hill above us.'

'This isn't hunting season, and if it was, this is certainly not hunting grounds.'

'Not for animals anyway,' I said as the second shot hit a tree near us. 'What's over that hill?'

Dani thought for a second. 'The main road. The skating rink is down there. Somebody could have come up there.'

'Unlikely. If somebody's been following us then he wouldn't know what path we took unless he watched us take this one. Then he could have skirted round the hill until he guessed where we would be.'

A third shot rang out and the bullet hit the undergrowth. I stepped out and fired off three rounds. That's when I saw the figure running through the trees. Just a glimpse, a figure wearing what looked like camouflage clothes. Dark hair. Running, about a couple of hundred yards away.

'He's up there, Dani. I'm going after him!'

'I'll take the path.'

She took off running as I started racing uphill through the trees and undergrowth, keeping one eye on where I was going, and the other on the top of the hill, in case he came back. I realized I was a sitting duck if he decided to stop and come back, but I had a feeling he was trying to get away after unsuccessfully trying to shoot me.

I didn't think Dani was the target, not after me getting the note the previous night.

As I reached the brow of the hill, I held my gun out, but there was nobody there.

There was a path running down the hill. Maybe used by joggers, or those on a mountain bike, but whatever it was, it was being used by the man who had taken a shot at us.

I ran. There was no choice. I could have been running into an ambush of course, but it was a chance I was prepared to take.

Going downhill, the trees were only on my left.

Open grassland was on my right and I could see the main road.

Ahead of me was the parking lot. There was no sign of the man. Cars were coming in whilst others were leaving.

A black Jeep Wrangler turned right and passed me by in the distance, driving away on the main road. I looked to see if the driver was wearing camo, but he was wearing a bright green t-shirt.

I stood at the side of a car, my breath coming and going rapidly, but thankfully my own jogging regime back home had got me prepared.

I looked around at the cars. Interspersed with the sedans were SUVs, a couple of minivans and a Ford F350 on steroids, the tires huge and the suspension lifted.

No sign of a man in camo gear.

Dani came running up behind me. 'Any sign?' she said, bending to lean on her knees.

'I think somebody needs to hit the treadmill more often,' I said, glancing at her for a moment. 'But no, there's no sign. He could have just left. There's been a few cars leaving.'

'I'm calling it in now.'

I looked around, just in case he was hiding, but I couldn't see anybody vaguely resembling him. Some young couple, a family with kids. A man with a walking cane at the back of his conversion van, giving his dog a drink of water.

He'd got a good head start on us so he was probably out on the road by now. But why take the chance? It was broad daylight. He had to be supremely confident of getting away.

I knew then that this was a warning, just like the note. Nobody else had been on this path. Two things came to mind. If he'd wanted to kill us, he could have walked up closer for a better shot. He'd have had a fifty-fifty chance of taking us out if he got up close. And he knew the place. Knew to take this path when he saw us walking down the other trail.

He had been following us, but had blended in. Which wouldn't have been hard at this time of year, with tourist buses coming into town, and visitor's cars overloading the parking lots.

'I called the Chief. They're on their way now.'

'You okay, Dani?'

'Yeah. I've been shot at before, just not up here. The Bronx was a whole different ballgame but it toughens you up. Still, I wish I'd got a shot off at him.'

The air cracked with the sound of sirens. I moved Dani to one side as the conversion van backed out. The old fella waved at us as he slowly pulled out and the team arrived.

'Christ, what happened?' Nikki Hunter said as she

leapt out of her car as the patrol cars skidded in behind and around her.

Dani explained what had happened.

'And you didn't see anybody fitting his description?' she said to me, her tone not far from accusing.

I wanted to tell her that yes, I did indeed see somebody fitting his description but decided to just let him get in his car and drive off, but I bit my tongue. 'No, Chief, there was nobody like him around when I got here.'

'Why in God's name would anybody take a potshot at you?'

'To scare me off. Just like the note from last night.'

'It sounds like he was trying to kill you both, not scare you.'

'He could have got up close but he didn't. He wasn't going for a kill shot. He wants to put the wind up me.'

Tourists were standing watching the show.

'Did you get a good look at him?' Nikki looked at me like I was hiding something.

'Dark hair. White. Wearing a camo jacket, maybe a hoody, maybe a rain jacket. And he could move, that's for sure.'

'Clearly, if he could get down here and leave before you got here.'

'He had a head start.' I mentally kicked myself for

sounding like I was defending myself.

'I'll get forensics on it. I already have patrol cars at either end of town on the main road, but I'm not holding out much hope.'

'There's nothing to find. One bullet took a chunk out of a tree before disappearing into the undergrowth. He obviously followed us here and watched which way we went before cutting us off. He knows this place.'

'He's a local for sure?'

'I would say so. This is not his first time up here, remember? He knows how to navigate round here.'

'What do you make of him?' There was a fine line of sweat on her brow and it wasn't from the sun overhead.

'I don't think he's finished.' Despite the summer heat, I felt cold inside. 'I think he's playing with us and he's going to leave us more corpses.'

What I didn't want to tell her just then was, I didn't think Tom Morgan was our killer. I had then, but not now. I hadn't got a good look at the man at the top of the hill, but the gun was unmistakable.

He was shooting with a revolver.

Just like the one he shot me with, back then.

As I stood looking back at the trees, I was picturing the man shooting at us. I knew then we hadn't got our killer four years ago.

And I thought he was back.

SIX

The forensics team were from the New York State Police. The Chief wanted to cover all bases, but I knew they'd find nothing. Unless the guy had left behind a cigarette with his DNA on it, but I don't think he was that stupid.

'Are you okay?' Dani asked me. I wondered what I looked like to make her ask that.

'I'm fine. You?'

'I've had better days. But did you notice that nobody seemed panicked when we came down? Like nobody heard the gunfire.'

'The other side of the hill would have blocked the sound from travelling so far. But I didn't get to see what we came here for. Namely the grave.'

One of the uniforms had brought a trailer with two

ATVs on it. Standard procedure round here I guessed. Make quick headway into the woods.

'Do you think they'd let you use one? You can drive.'

'I don't see why not.'

Two minutes' conversation with the Chief and both the vehicles were unloaded and four of us headed up the hill. Not the Chief, but two detectives called Simms and Hope.

I held onto Dani as she shot the vehicle up the hill, followed by the other two. We reached the point where the gunman had fired at us and carried on past. The path was rough but the ATV took it in its stride.

The trees provided shade once more as we went further into the woods. I caught glimpses of the construction in the distance as we zipped down to meet the path with the crushed stone.

Five minutes later, we arrived at the grave site where Sofia had been left. It had remnants of crime scene tape.

We stopped the ATV, the others right behind us.

I looked around us. There was significant cover from the trees, although the path was open. The grave was maybe twenty feet in from the path.

'He's confident, I'll give him that,' Hope said.

'Most certainly a local,' Simms added, although we

all thought that anyway. Or at least it was somebody with local knowledge.

'Nobody saw anything at all?' I said, nodding to the makeshift grave.

'Nothing,' Dani answered. 'We reckon he did it after dark.'

'There are no CCTV cameras at the parking lot?'

'No. These are hiker's trails. There's no need for any cameras here. It isn't the Bronx,' Simms said.

I ignored him and looked down into the makeshift grave.

'How can anybody have dug a grave here and nobody saw him?' the older detective said again. 'He was a cocky son of a bitch.'

I stood looking over to the pathway. The grave was about twenty feet in. Nobody could have missed him if they had been walking by. It had to have been dug in the dark, but the park is closed after sunset, the metal barrier across the driveway, locked with a padlock. Maybe he had done it close to sunset and then left on foot, but there wasn't any parking near the outside of the park because of drainage ditches.

There was one possible explanation I could think of; he had come here first light. With a partner. One digs, one keeps a lookout. I realized we must be looking for two people, which would explain why he was able to get away easily. He could have gotten in the back of a car and ducked down and I wouldn't have seen him.

We went back down to where the Chief was. I kept my thoughts to myself.

The parking lot had been cleared of public cars now, no more allowed in. 'Forensics are still running the victim's clothes. At least we have a name for her. But that just adds to the complications, a victim we didn't know about.'

'It might be unconnected,' I said to her. 'The killings were all over the media, so it's not a wild guess to think that somebody might have discovered just her.'

'You think she was murdered and dumped somewhere away from the others?'

'They might all be dumped far apart, but that's not what I would say. He would want to contain the area where he kept them. But we can't discount the idea that this is another murder made to look like the victim of Tom Morgan.' I couldn't think of the real killer by his media name, *The Gravedigger*. It was my opinion that this only served to give them celebrity status, whether they wanted it or not.

'Or he might have gone on a rampage and killed a lot more women than we thought, and now this sicko has them and is playing games with us,' Dani said.

'It could go either way.'

Nikki Hunter looked pale. 'I wish this was a one-horse town where the only problems were a couple of drunks on a Saturday night.'

'I told Scott I'm going to call my ex who's with the NYPD and have him deal with the death message. He can talk to the family, get some more background on her.'

Hunter nodded and walked back over to her cruiser.

SEVEN

Dani and I went over to her folk's place. Atticus jumped all over me as if he thought I'd taken him to a kennel and wasn't coming back. I rubbed his back as he spun round and round.

'He's missed you,' Bill said. We were out in one of the enclosures, watching the horses in another. Two of them. They were beautiful big beasts, but I had an irrational fear of them. Nothing I could put my finger on but I felt myself going tense whenever I was near one, which wasn't often.

'I missed him.'

'So, who was she?' Bill asked me.

I thought for a moment he was talking about the victim, but then I realized he wasn't.

'The woman who broke your heart,' he elaborated.

I looked across at the horses. The sun was beginning to clip the tress on the edge of the property but it was still warm.

'Nobody. I haven't had anybody special in my life for a long time.' Not quite the truth, but I didn't want to go into it. There were some women who stayed longer than others, but in the last four years, there hadn't been anybody around to break my heart.

'Dinner's ready!' Dani shouted from the kitchen door at the back of the house.

I turned and smiled and waved. Atticus ran towards her.

Bill put a hand on my shoulder and we started walking towards the house. 'Danielle's been hurt, Scott,' he said to me. 'Her ex-husband fooled around on her. I don't like him. I wouldn't let him set foot on my property. He would get introduced to my twelve-gauge if he did.'

'Dani's a tough girl,' I said.

'She is now. She wasn't back then. Oh, it's water under the bridge now, and I'm sure she shows off that tough exterior to people, but I know my little girl.'

'I don't think she'll let anybody hurt her again.' I tried to keep the redness from creeping into my face but I was sure I'd failed.

Atticus had scooted through the door and was inside.

'Sometimes it's hard to see when you're looking

69

through *love eyes*, as her mom calls them. She might carry a gun, but she has feelings like everybody else.'

The lecture was thinly veiled. 'Bill, if you're worried that I might take advantage of Dani, I can assure you—'

We stopped and he cut me short. 'She's a big girl. Old enough to make her own decisions. But she'll always be *my* little girl. And I will always look out for her.'

'I can always move out and find somewhere with the dog.'

He smiled again. 'No need for that. As long as we know where the line in the sand is.'

I smiled back at him. 'I know where it is, Bill.'

'Good man. Let's go eat.'

Inside, the smell of freshly baked bread filled the kitchen, as if they were planning to sell the farmhouse and were trying to attract a buyer.

A salad was in a bowl in the middle of the table, with hot potatoes in another. Dani turned and smiled at me as I entered. I sneaked a quick peak at Bill, but he wasn't looking at me. Probably wondering if he'd remembered to load his shotgun.

'This looks fantastic, Dr Fox,' I said. Sylvia had been a surgeon before retirement. If I hadn't known her age, I would have thought she was a much younger woman.

'Thank you,' she said, turning from the counter where she and her daughter were adding some meats to the plates. 'And I've told you before, it's *Sylvia*.'

There was a jug of cold lemonade on the table. We sat down when the plates were put down and the warm bread was brought out of the oven. Bill said grace.

'Danielle told me you're still in Newburgh,' Sylvia said as she dished out some salad onto her plate.

'Yes. It's my home town. I was done with Washington.'

'It must have been hard leaving the FBI,' Bill said as he filled his own plate and passed the bowl to me. The potatoes were making the rounds from the other direction.

'I was offered medical retirement. On account of my knee. And the bullet still lodged near my spine. They got the rest but one of them got too comfortable, and surgery would be too dangerous to remove it.'

'Do you like lecturing?' Sylvia asked. She seemed genuinely interested, unlike some people who thought that being a PI and a lecturer was a big step down from hunting serial killers with the feds.

'The kids are great, to be honest. Most of them come from Long Island and New Jersey, with well-to-do families, and although they can be boisterous at times, they're a good bunch.'

Dani and I swapped bowls, salad for potatoes.

'How about the private eye business?' Bill asked, tucking into his food.

'I suppose that was me not quite wanting to let go of being involved in law enforcement in some form. I don't do a lot of PI work, to be honest. I get by on my pension and my pay.'

Atticus lay down on the floor near Dani. I buttered a slice of bread, looking over at Dani. She gave me a quick glance and a sly smile, as if we were at the family table and I was one of the farm hands, and she had taken me as her secret lover.

It made me feel good inside. It had been so long since I was in the company of a beautiful woman. I poured some lemonade and filled the other glasses.

'How are you finding retirement, Bill?' I asked.

'He's grumpy most of the time,' Sylvia said, laughing.

'He asked *me*,' Bill said.

'See? What did I tell you?'

'I can answer for myself.' Then he looked at me. 'I'm grumpy most of the time.' He and Sylvia both laughed. 'To be honest, I thought I'd be comfortable with it, not having to get up early on a freezing winter morning or getting called out in the middle of the night when there was an auto accident. But I miss it. I guess we're both in the same position, almost.'

'How about you, Sylvia?' I asked.

'I miss being a surgeon, but then I became Director of Nursing after that. Wielding a pen wasn't the same as wielding a scalpel. Now I just volunteer, helping out as a caregiver to elderly folks.'

'Everybody dreams of retirement,' Bill said, 'but when it gets here, you think, *What now?*'

'You must have mixed feelings about coming here,' Sylvia said, her voice soft. 'You came back here three years ago, looking for Jessie. And now you're here again.'

'It makes me feel sad,' I said to her. 'Guilty, too, if I'm honest.'

'You can't feel guilty about that, son,' Bill said.

'You took five bullets, Scott,' Dani said, and reached over to squeeze my hand. I didn't look at Bill for fear of my face turning bright red. 'Plus the one that grazed your head.'

'I should have gone with her that night. I didn't. And I never saw her again.'

'Then I hope we get the answers we're looking for,' Dani said.

We ate for a bit and made small talk.

'Sylvia and I were thinking of going to Europe for a trip, sometime soon,' Bill said. 'I have Irish blood in me somewhere.'

'Me too,' I said. 'My grandmother's father was Irish.'

'You have family over there now?' Sylvia asked.

'I have an aunt who lives there. My mother's Scottish.'

'Oh, that's fascinating. I do ancestry and I've gone back quite a ways, and I found out that my great-great-grandfather came from the Scottish Highlands. So, we both have Scottish blood in us.'

'I'll raise my glass to that,' I said, and we clinked glasses and laughed.

'Are your folks still around?' she asked.

'No. They moved down to Florida after my dad retired. He was a cop. He did his twenty-five years and now spends his time fishing with some new buddies he met down there. They love it, although it's a bit humid for my mom at times.'

'Family is everything,' Bill said, no longer smiling. He shared a look with his wife.

The night ended on a high note, with Bill cracking open a new bottle of 25-year old Scotch. I declined his offer. I had the odd beer, but I always wanted to be alert. I told myself it was in case Atticus suddenly took ill and I needed to take him to the vet, but deep down, I knew that being drunk would mean letting my guard down, and I'd promised myself that would never happen again.

Atticus lay down in the back of the car as Dani drove us home.

The dog ran into the house like it was his own, but then he ran to the back door and stood barking and growling.

'What is it, boy?' I switched the light off and looked out through the glass. The fur was up on the back of his neck. I grabbed his leash and opened the door.

'What's wrong?' Dani asked, concern on her face as she saw Atticus.

'He sees something.' I didn't patronize her by telling her something stupid like *Stay here,* and was pleased with the way she drew her gun out.

'Let's go,' she said.

We stepped out into her backyard, which was a considerable size. Atticus growled and tugged on the leash as he pulled me towards the trees. I drew my own gun. If somebody was there and a mouth full of sharp teeth didn't get him, then a 9mm would.

We entered the tree line, Dani keeping abreast, the flashlight on her gun shining into the trees. There was nothing obvious. I turned around to make sure we had shut the back door. We had.

Atticus kept on pulling, up the incline. On the other side, we stopped, all three of us and looked at the sight before us.

At the woman hanging from the tree.

EIGHT

There was a scream from the woods. 'Here, take Atticus,' I said to Dani as he launched into a tirade of growling and barking. I slipped the leash off my wrist and handed it to her.

'Scott, for God's sake. Stay here. I'll call it in.'

I took off running. 'Do that, call it in!' I shouted, the beam from my flashlight bouncing off trees and branches. I knew we had driven up the road that was on the west side of her house and I suddenly darted that way. Straight ahead was the lake, and I knew that if somebody was trying to get away, he'd either come by boat – which I doubted – or he had parked at the side of the road near somebody's property.

I was hoping the scream was coming from a neighbor seeing the killer and not because she had become a victim.

My feet thudded on the dirt floor. I saw light through the trees and knew there was a possibility that my light would give my position away. Like World War II, when the dead man was the third one to take a light from the match. The first strike letting the sniper know of their position. The second giving him a fix on where to aim. The third man a sitting duck as the sniper pulled the trigger.

I put my flashlight out, cursing myself for not coming in here in the darkness. My eyes took a few moments to start adjusting to the dark, branches whipping at my face. It was overgrown here, the vegetation thick.

I was getting closer to the house lights of Dani's neighbor. I burst through the trees and landed in their side yard. The woman screamed again just as her husband turned with the shotgun and chambered a round.

I threw my hands up, illuminated by their security lights. 'FBI! FBI!' I shouted. 'Don't shoot!'

The man looked skeptical at first, but held the gun out in front of him, and I could tell by his stance that he wouldn't hesitate to use it.

'Keep your hands where I can see them!'

I lowered my hands to waist height. 'Did you see somebody come through here?' I said.

'Yes!' the woman answered, clearly shaken. 'Somebody dressed in black, wearing a ski mask. He came out of the woods, ran across my lawn then into the woods again. The dog started barking and when I came to look, he came out of the trees.'

'Show me your badge,' her husband said, just as the first police cruiser screeched to a halt at the end of their driveway.

'Put the gun down!' the officer shouted, just as another car pulled in behind. An unmarked Crown Vic.

The householder put his gun down. 'He's the one you want! He just ran into our yard.'

'Everybody relax,' Chief Nikki Hunter said, walking over. 'Marshall, put your hands down.'

'You know this guy?' the homeowner said. 'He told us he's with the FBI.'

Nikki looked at me and I could swear she rolled her eyes. 'He's a consultant. He's with us now. Tell me what happened here.'

I stood close by, looking around but I didn't see anybody hiding out in the dark woods. The woman repeated what she had just told me.

'Which way did he go?'

'Back into the woods.'

Nikki turned to some uniforms as more patrol cars stopped. 'Get the house searched. Just in case.'

'Dani's round at her own house with the dog. You need to get men round there as well.'

'They're already there. I was on my way there when this call came in.' She looked at me. 'Get in my car. We're going round there now.'

I did as she said and sat beside her in the front. 'Somebody's going out their way to warn you off. Any ideas who?'

'None at all,' I said as she drove away and headed round to Dani's. She was there, standing talking to a patrol officer, Atticus by her side. 'I called the medical examiner. He's coming out. So are the State Police forensics crew.'

'You said there's a body in the woods?' Nikki said, as if hearing about it the first time had been a nightmare and now she was discovering that it wasn't.

'A young woman. Hanging by her neck. Dressed in a shroud.'

'Jesus.' She looked at me as if this was all my fault. 'Why do you think somebody wants you to leave town?'

I thought the answer was pretty simple, but didn't voice that opinion. 'Whoever was involved four years ago, doesn't want me being here because they know Jessie was my partner.'

'Tom Morgan was involved four years ago. Are you

saying he was working with somebody?' Her face took on a twisted look, somewhere between fear and anger.

'Somebody knows the connection between me and Jessie. They're warning me off. Whoever it is who found the bodies. They're not going to stop.'

'*They*? Tell me you're using that in a general sense of the word.'

I shook my head. 'No. I think there's more than one of them. I don't know if just one person found the corpses, but there's more than one of them working to display them.'

'I don't believe it.'

Whether she believed it or not, I could care less. 'The neighbor we just spoke to? She said her dog alerted her to a noise, like there was somebody in her backyard. I think that was the first one running through. Then when she opened her back door, the second one was running across her yard.'

'That's just speculation.'

'That's what I used to get paid for; speculating. But there's more than that to worry about; whoever displayed the first body has upped their game. They're now cold-blooded killers.'

Despite the darkness, I could see the color leave her face. 'What are you talking about?'

Dani stepped forward. 'There's blood all around

the neck area where the victim's hanging. This isn't somebody who was killed years ago.'

'Somebody's carrying on Tom Morgan's legacy?' Nikki said, her voice sounding raspy and dry.

'Go and look for yourself,' I said, noncommittally. She turned and walked away across Dani's backyard, the security lights doing a good job with the illumination.

More people were turning up, like it was some macabre party. Technicians, State Police, and Dani's father, Bill.

'Thanks for coming, Dad,' Dani said. 'Atticus is getting excited with all the people coming and going.'

'No problem. But what's going on?'

Dani told him about the body in the woods.

'Any idea who it is?'

'It still has a shroud on. And this isn't one of the old victims; there's blood seeping through it. And a previous victim wouldn't have blood coming from her, would she?'

Bill made a face at her. 'How many times did you accompany me to the morgue when you were younger? How many questions you asked me?'

She grinned. 'That was for Scott's sake.'

'Oh yeah, bring me into this.'

'It means you have a murder victim on your hands, but if her face is covered, then you aren't going to be able to identify her until forensics have been over the area.'

I stepped back out of the way of a tech going by with equipment. 'Your neighbor said the man who came into her yard ran into the woods. Where could he have gone if he didn't come back here?'

'There's a trail that runs along the edge of the lake. It comes out at the Arrow Lake country club on the north end.'

'I want to go along it. First light tomorrow. First though, I want to go and speak to somebody.'

We watched the crews working in the woods, and I wondered, not for the first time, who saw me as a threat.

NINE

Nikki Hunter unclipped her badge and side holster, making sure the gun was within easy reach.

The first body had given her chills, not because of the viciousness of it all, but because of the files.

The ones she kept in her study. It was no longer a room with a desk and a computer, but more of a shrine. If she were to go and see a therapist, he or she might tell Nikki that she had an unhealthy obsession, but she would counter with, *you haven't seen the wall in my study*.

She stood looking at it now. News clippings from the killings and the abductions from four years ago. Long before she came back to town to take over the role of Chief.

The clippings were from newspapers in the area

and further afield. Clippings her father had collected. He'd only been in the ground six months, but it felt a lot longer. Would she look back on this years from now, and think that the time that had passed seemed a lot longer? It felt that way when she thought about her mother's death. Twelve years, but when she thought about it, it seemed like a whole lifetime had passed.

Nikki had always been a daddy's girl. He had encouraged her to become a police officer, but she had wanted to get out of this town and be an officer somewhere else. So, she had chosen Rochester and had gone through the academy. Her father had been proud. What he hadn't been so proud of was her choice of man to marry.

It was like he had been looking into a crystal ball. Dan Hunter had been rotten to the core. Nikki hadn't seen it, blinded by love. She had gone ahead and married him despite her father's fears. It had lasted a little more than a year. Dan always had been a smooth talker, with an eye for the women. It was how he had captured Nikki. She had foolishly thought he would settle down after he was married, but that hadn't happened.

A young despatcher had caught his eye and fallen for his charms. She had caught him in their bed with the young girl. That had been the end of it. Dan moved out of the house, out of the police department, out of the state, last time she heard. She didn't know if he had ended up with the pretty little thing, and she didn't want to know.

Her father never once said *I told you so.*

Nikki had stayed with the department in Rochester, where nobody from the town knew she had a failed marriage, and her life revolved around her job.

She had dated but none of them had worked out. It was purely physical and none of them matched her expectations.

She stood staring at the faces of the woman who was now confirmed dead and the others missing presumed dead. Two victims were displayed to be found, four years ago, and four other women reported missing, all around the same age, and they believed they were the work of the serial killer. The four were still missing. Sofia Martinez's name wasn't even known to them back then.

Her father's words still rang in her head. *Nikki, you need to come home. I know who killed them.*

Her rapid-fire questions right after that had gone unanswered. It was the most coherent thing he had said on the phone to her. She'd always known her father liked a drink, but it hadn't stopped him from doing his job as chief of police.

That night, more than six months ago, had chilled her to the bone. It had taken her over five hours to drive from Rochester up to Arrow Lake. By the time she got there, her father had already been pronounced dead and was in the morgue in the hospital.

Amongst his possessions, she had found the old trunk. It had all the old newspaper clippings from when the killings took place. She knew it had taken a toll on her father. The old man had seen it as a failure on his part. But the forces behind the murders were more than anybody could take on alone.

Nikki at down on the chair she kept in here, her *thinking* chair. She was convinced that the answer was here somewhere.

Everybody had thought that Tom Morgan was their killer, including her, but something had made her father think otherwise. She sat with a drink in her hand. This was her nightly routine now and had been since she had applied for and got the job as Chief.

Magnus Porter had welcomed her to the town. He had known her since she was a little girl and she was sure that he had had influence with the town board when it came to hiring new police officers.

Her father felt he had let the town – and Magnus – down. Nikki knew he hadn't, but she wanted to carry on her father's legacy. She wasn't going to let anyone down.

The knock at her door broke her reverie.

'Have you ever been here before?' I asked Dani as we got out of the car. I'd parked on the street, directly outside the house. It was a tidy Craftsman style with a well-kept yard out front.

'No,' Dani answered as she locked her Tahoe and we walked up to Nikki Hunter's front door.

The Chief answered it quickly. She'd been expecting us and I thought for a moment that she'd been standing behind the door, waiting to yank it open.

'Come in,' she said, standing aside. There wasn't a smile offered, nor one expected.

She closed the door and led us through to the kitchen at the back of the house. 'Coffee?' she said. 'Something stronger?'

'Coffee's fine,' I said, and Dani nodded.

Nikki scuttled about. Her coffee pot was already on as if she'd anticipated our answer. Mugs filled, we sat at the kitchen table.

'Thank you for coming, Scott,' she finally said. 'You too, Dani. Call me Nikki. This isn't a formal meeting.'

'Anything we can do to help,' I told her, not rushing her to get to the point. This woman ran a police department. I didn't think she would need rushing.

'You know, protocol would be for me to ask you to leave town,' she said, her hands grasping the mug like it was a hand grenade she'd just pulled the pin from and now couldn't find.

'But?' I said.

'But, I think that's what the killer wants. He's sending you messages to leave, because he knows there's a good chance you'll catch him.'

'I didn't catch him before. He caught *me*. But I know you mean this new guy.' I felt that the killer had more confidence in me than I did.

'You obviously have the wind up him. You said you thought he was just sending you a message on the trail in the park. I disagree. I think he tried to take you out and when that didn't work, he's trying a new way to get you to leave.'

'*They*,' Dani said. 'There's more than one. And they proved it tonight.'

'I agree. The thing that's getting me is, why would they start killing now, if all they had done so far was found the corpses from four years ago and were only displaying them for kicks? The answer is simple; we didn't get him four years ago. Yes, Detective Tom Morgan took his own life, and the town thought they'd caught *The Gravedigger*.' She looked at us in turn. 'Who came up with that godawful name anyway?'

'The gutter press,' Dani said.

They didn't have a new President to take up all their time back then.'

'Anyway, I don't think we got the right man back then, and he's back. What I don't know, is why now.' She drank some of the coffee and waited for our objections, getting none.

'I agree,' I said.

'I know. That's why, when I was driving you round to Dani's tonight, I asked you to come around here. And bring Dani if she feels the same way. Now, I see you do.'

'I do,' Dani said, her coffee sitting untouched in front of her. 'What's convinced you?'

Nikki paused before carrying on. 'My father. He called me the day he died and told me he knew who had killed them, back then. He wouldn't tell me on the phone, so I drove five hours to get here from Rochester. By the time I arrived in town, he was dead. Hit-and-run. They thought it was a drunk driver, but I knew it wasn't. My father was getting close to whoever was responsible and he was killed.'

'Chief Walker was a great man,' Dani said. 'He was the one who promoted me.'

'He always had good things to say about you,' Nikki said. 'He thought you brought a lot to the department, coming from NYC.'

'I was brought up in Brooklyn, Chief. We stayed

with my grandmother in her house, until my dad took the job as ME up here.'

'I thought you were born up here,' I said.

She shook her head. 'No, we kept the house after grandma died, then I moved into it when I worked down there. We still have it. Renters are in it just now.'

'Chief Walker saw the potential in you,' I said.

'I do too,' Nikki said, 'but I'm not going to be here long enough to promote you through the ranks. I need you to keep this to yourself, but I only came here to find out who killed my father, and I think it's the same person who is killing now, and who killed before.'

'How can you be so sure?' Dani asked.

Nikki let go of her mug and stood up. 'Come with me.'

We followed her through to a bedroom where all the clippings and papers were stuck on cork boards. 'This was my dad's stuff. He had collected it all. He and Tom Morgan were close. I mean, real close. Tom was like a son to him. That's why my dad didn't believe we had the right man, back then. He voiced an opinion to Washington, but they blew him off as some stupid old small-town cop.'

'I never heard the Chief say that,' I told her, 'not even when I came back a year after the event.'

'He didn't voice it to anybody but the feds, when it happened. He didn't know who he could trust.

Then one weekend, I came home for a visit. I had split with my husband, and I just needed to get away for a break. My dad had been drinking and he told me how much he missed Tom. He couldn't believe Tom was a killer.

'He said that Tom was only on their radar because he had once had an affair with one of the victims. But that was no reason to suspect him. Tom was his own worst enemy. He always had an eye for the ladies.'

'I started to doubt myself when I was in the hospital, recovering,' I said. 'They flew me down to Westchester Medical Center. I was there for six weeks. Plenty of time to think.'

'What was it you doubted?' Nikki asked me.

'I was shot five times, but one bullet had grazed my forehead. Not life threatening, but it was enough for blood to run down my face and join the tears that had formed after he shot me another five times. He stood right above me, pointing the gun. I couldn't make out his face but I always thought this man was stockier than Tom Morgan. And I could swear he didn't have a moustache. Morgan did.'

Dani was hanging on my every word. Then she looked at Nikki. 'Let's assume this wasn't Morgan for a moment; why would Morgan have taken his own life?'

'That's the thing, Dani. I don't think he did. I think whoever was killing, was discovered by Morgan, or he was lured to that cabin. I think they got him there and killed him. Case closed.'

'Why would they use him?' Dani said.

'To take any heat off the real killer. It's possible he thought to cool things down. Maybe he's stopped killing until now, or he killed elsewhere. Whatever it was, he's started here again.'

TEN

'You look shattered,' Dani said to me as the sun was rising above the treetops.

It looked like the circus was in town, only they were driving police cruisers and other vehicles with spinning, colored lights, in a very patriotic red, white, and blue.

'And you look like you've had a full eight hours,' I said, realizing that it sounded sarcastic. 'I meant that as a compliment,' I added.

'I know you did. Where's Atticus?'

'Inside with a tech. probably chewing a piece of expensive equipment.' He barked, as if he knew we were talking about him and he was voicing an opinion. Bill couldn't take him. He had a few bits and pieces he wanted to take out the cabin before the keys were handed over to the new owner.

I was sitting at the patio table, my millionth cup of coffee in front of me, my phone sitting looking back at me. I had brought up the photo of the note again, each time hoping that I had read it wrong the time before. But I hadn't.

Go home, Scott.

'The tech says that it could have been printed off any printer in anybody's house, anywhere in America,' Dani said, looking at the photo on my phone.

'Not anywhere in America; somewhere here, in Arrow Lake.'

'It's a laser printer anyway. A cheap one that can be bought anywhere.'

She moved from behind me and sat down with her own coffee. 'Somebody has to be watching us. They know you're staying here.'

'You have video surveillance, but you didn't get a notice on your phone that it had been set off last night. And he was careful to stay over the brow of the hill so he wouldn't set it off.'

'And there are hiking trails that run from the lake up to near where he left her.'

'How would he get here up the trail? Could only be by ATV,' I said, answering my own question.

'I don't understand why he wants you to go. You came back here a year after the murders and nothing.

Now you're back after one of the victims is displayed, and suddenly he's sending you a message.'

I looked at her. The morning air was a bit chilly and it was only now that I was feeling it. 'He thinks I know something. And he doesn't really expect me to leave. It's a warning, of what he's doing. He's moved on from telling me to go home, to giving a message that he's coming for me.'

'The killing starting again?'

'It's designed to add confusion to the mix. It will get the people at the top to stop and think about it; *will the killings start again? If Scott Marshall goes home, will all of this disappear?* That sort of thing.'

'It's not going away though, Scott. He displayed Sophia before you were even here.'

'I know. I've been thinking about this all night. I think, despite what the note says, that he wants me here. It was a long shot that I would come back, but it was fifty-fifty that I would, after the first one was displayed.' I drank some coffee and looked at her.

'He wants you here, doesn't he?' she said, her voice a little above a whisper.

I nodded. 'Despite what he's saying and doing, he wants me right here. He sees it as a challenge.'

'I think your life is in danger. I think maybe you should go back to Newburgh.'

'I'm not going anywhere.'

'I asked you to come here. I don't know how I would handle it if the killer now singled you out and something happened.'

'It's a hazard that comes with the job. But I think that now he sees me here, he wants me around. Maybe he's going to try and make me the scapegoat.'

'Let me ask you; when we were looking for the killer four years ago, was Tom Morgan on your radar before he became a suspect?' she asked me.

'No. I was surprised when they said they were looking for him. I had spoken to Tom before that day, and he never gave off any vibes that he was their man.'

'Did Jessie think he was the killer?'

I thought about it for a moment. 'I don't think so. I don't recall her saying she thought it was him.'

'I wonder what he's been doing for four years. If it isn't just somebody who happened to find the bodies? If it is really somebody who was involved in the original killings?'

'The usual answers that the FBI profilers give; he moved away and now he's back, he could have been in prison. Something made him go away for four years and now he's returned. But it also leaves us with another unanswered question; we figured out there's more than one guy involved, so who's the other person working with him?'

'I wish we could definitively say it wasn't Tom Morgan.'

Dani drank some of her own coffee. Her eyes looked tired. Like me, she had dozed off in one of the chairs in the living room while Atticus lay beside me. The techs worked outside all night.

'It's not certain it wasn't Tom Morgan. Everything pointed to him, back then, so this might be a copycat,' I said.

'You don't believe that any more than I do.'

I nodded, agreeing with her. 'They set up Morgan, and he took the fall. Now I'm back in town, and I have a feeling that they're going to use me. I wasn't part of their original plan, obviously, but now they see I'm here, I have a feeling that they're going to suck me in somehow. This is not the work of one man. I'd put money on it.'

One of the detectives came over to us. 'Dani? There's something up with the body.' He looked at me and I felt like I had fallen down an elevator shaft. He was just about to blow our theory out of the water.

'It could be one of our previous victims. She's badly decomposed.' He paused for effect, maybe waiting to see if we could guess what was coming next.

I had first go. 'There's fresh blood on the shroud.'

He nodded. It felt like we were on a game show.

'Blood was put on the shroud before the girl was hauled up into the tree.'

'He's sending us a message,' Dani said. 'He put fresh blood on it, telling us he's killed somebody else.'

'We need her identity as soon as,' I said to the other detective.

'They're cutting her down now. She's being taken to the morgue. We'll find out soon enough.'

ELEVEN

The morning air would have been heavier had we not been down by the lake, which off threw a light breeze. Atticus was the only one out of the three of us who had eaten that morning. We had showered and changed into fresh clothes. Once again, I felt something inside tug at me when I looked at Dani.

The night we had spent together, three years ago in her parents' cabin, I hadn't asked about her background, her private life, and she hadn't asked me either. It had been a night where we had taken solace in each other's company.

I had gone home to my housekeeper, and my thoughts of a beautiful woman who lived three hours away. I knew she would be able to find anybody she wanted. I had been surprised when she told me she didn't have a regular lover in her life.

'Do you believe in destiny?' she asked me as we walked round the trail, heading east.

I stopped and Atticus looked at me with his ears up, as if waiting for me to point out the bogey man. I rubbed the side of his head just below his left ear as he faced me.

'I hadn't really thought about it. Why do you ask?'

She shrugged and smiled. 'No reason. Just one of those fleeting thoughts that goes through your mind.'

I smiled at her, despite the seriousness of the situation.

We were on the trail that went right round the lake. It didn't seem that big when looked at on a map, but it was big enough. We could see jet skis and boats further out. We were under a canopy of trees and the shade felt good.

'They could have come this way,' I said, talking about the men from the night before, 'but I don't think they would head towards town. I think they would head that way.' I pointed to the northwest side of the lake where the houses were being built. The same houses that I had seen yesterday, from the top of the trail where Sophia Martinez had been found.

'The new country club.' Dani shook her head. 'Those houses are going to go for a fortune. Plus, they'll get free membership to the club. I saw the plans in the town hall when they had a preview night.' She turned to look at me. 'For the great unwashed like me. They had a ball at the present club, where the rich and famous go. We had sandwiches, they had lobster no doubt.'

'Old man Porter always gets what he wants, I guess.'

'Every time.'

I looked back at the trail heading west. 'Your neighbor last night gave a statement to your officers. She didn't hear any engine starting up after the man ran through her yard. I know the woods are on a hill, which gives you and her a windbreak from the lake, but on a quiet night, there should have been some noise heard.'

'You think they left on foot?'

'No, I think they had some sort of quieter vehicle.'

'Like what?'

'What do they have at a country club?'

'Golf carts.'

'Let's take a drive round.'

We walked back up through the woods. There were still plenty of people around, techs and uniformed officers. I hoped they'd lock up when they were finished.

We took Dani's Tahoe, the air inside cold after she had remotely started it from her phone. I gave Atticus a drink before he jumped into the car. I always carried a backpack with water in it for him.

'There has to be a reason why he killed somebody and put the blood on the shroud,' I said as she drove down the road and took a right at the main road, heading in the direction of the country club.

'Like you said, he was either killing somewhere else or in prison. Now he's back, and if he went away and had stored the bodies, then he wants to get rid of them so he can start again.'

'Good point. Did anything come back from corrections?'

'No. They haven't released anybody from around here.'

I had asked Dani to have her department connect with the department of corrections and see if any inmate was now free and heading back to the area. I'd thought it was a long shot and was proved right.

The *Arrow Lake Country Club* came up on our right, and Dani drove through the pillared gates and under a canopy of trees, down a long driveway until it opened out into a wide parking lot. Tennis courts were over to the left, and what looked like a very old building was straight ahead. The clubhouse itself.

We left the car running with the air conditioning on full blast, but I didn't like the idea of leaving Atticus for long. I'd read somewhere about the K9 dogs who died in hot police cars after the engine cut out.

We were shown inside, into the cool interior that could have been the inside of a baronial castle. It reeked of old money.

'Can I help you?' a young female said, walking up to us. Her smile was fixed in place, reserved for people who came in here who weren't recognized. She dressed in a skirt and blazer in the club's colors, a walkie-talkie in one hand.

'We'd like to speak with the head of security,' Dani said, showing her badge and introducing me.

'I can call him,' she said, raising the walkie-talkie to her mouth, but a voice came from behind her before she could speak.

'I can deal with this,' a tall man said, walking over to us.

'Oh, certainly, Mr Porter.' The woman smiled at him and left the entrance hall.

'Come through here and we'll get a coffee or something,' Porter said. 'Detective Fox isn't it?'

'Yes. This is Scott Marshall. He's a consultant with us.'

'Ay, yes, Mr Marshall. I remember you from the last time. I'm Raif Porter, Magnus's son.'

We followed him through into the members'

lounge, which was large and magnificent. It had a view directly over Arrow Lake.

'This is a very impressive club,' I said, massaging his ego.

'Yes, it is. The new one is going to be even better. Have you seen the plans?' Porter was acting like a tour guide.

'I've seen it at the town hall,' Dani said.

Porter looked at me, determined not to be put off.

'No, I'm new in town.'

'Then let me show you!' he said, beaming. We walked over to one end of the room, round by the end of the huge bar. There were plans on the walls, showing the site plan for the new homes that were being built on the ground that had been cleared on the opposite side of the lake. Phases one and two. Phase three was just highlighted.

'The new club is going to be bigger and more luxurious than this place,' he said. 'And, we can always do deals on houses for our special clients.' He grinned at Dani.

'We're here to talk about an incident last night,' Dani said, ignoring the barely-concealed attempt at, if not bribery, then favoritism.

'Okay. Let's get a seat.' He smiled as he walked away to one of the tables outside on the large patio. People were dining, and there was a buzz in the air. 'Would you like something to eat?'

'No, thank you,' Dani answered and I just shook my head as he looked at me.

'Allow me to get us some seltzer,' he said, turning to the waiter who had magically appeared at his side. He ordered three drinks and the waiter scuttled away.

'What happened last night that you need to come and talk to me about?' Porter said.

'I'm sure you heard about it on the news this morning; a woman was found hanging in the woods, up from the hiking trail. Just along from here.'

'Jeez, I most certainly did not hear about that. A woman hanging in the woods? That's awful.'

'She was one of the victims of *The Gravedigger*,' I said, studying every inch of his face for a reaction.

The waiter was back with the drinks.

There was a look of shock on Porter's face. A hint of red creeping into his cheeks. 'This guy I've been reading about, has displayed another corpse from the serial killer?' His eyebrows knotted very slightly and I could see him clenching his teeth.

'He has. We think he maybe used the hiking trail round the lake, taking her on a golf buggy. I believe there are ones that are used for utility purposes,' Dani said. 'Would you mind if we had a look around?'

Porter drank some of the cold drink and I took the

opportunity to sip some of my own. The heat was building up outside and we'd soon be back in the blazing sun.

'No, of course not. But it pains me to think that somebody would take one of our vehicles and use it for such a nefarious purpose. I'll personally take you to where they're kept and you can have access to anything.'

We all stood up. 'Thank you, Mr Porter,' I said.

'Call me Raif. And there's no need to thank me.'

'I have my dog in the car. I'd like to go and check on him.'

'What kind of dog?' he asked.

'German Shepherd. The Czechoslovakian kind, not the American style.'

'Beautiful dogs. If you follow me.'

He led us through to the reception area again. 'I'll catch up,' I said, heading for the exit.

Dani smiled and gave me the keys. Outside, the older clientele were arriving in their big boats-on-wheels. Some were carrying golf clubs, some tennis rackets. It reminded me to call my folks and promise them I'd be down to Florida soon to see them.

Atticus was pleased to see me and I took him over to a grassy area where he left his membership application. I put him back in the car, making sure the rear vents were blowing air on him, then caught up with

Dani at the other side of the club where she and Porter were looking at golf buggies and ATVs.

'These are the ones used by the staff,' Porter said unnecessarily. 'Could somebody have used this to transport a... corpse?' He indicated to a two-seater with a small pick-up bed at the back.

'Yes,' I answered, no doubt in my mind that two men could have used this. There were two machines like this. 'Do you have security cameras round here?'

'No. We have them covering the entrances of course, but there's nothing of value here and they're locked up behind a gate overnight.'

'I'd like to have a crew come over and fingerprint it, get it forensically checked out,' Dani said.

'Go ahead. I'm at your disposal, detective.'

We walked back into the cool of the building. 'Can I ask you; why is a new club being built? This one is superb,' I said.

We stopped and Porter looked at me. 'Size. This club was a house at one time, then it was expanded as demand for membership grew, then we realized that it just wasn't big enough for the future. My father owns land across on the other side, so we decided to build a new one.'

'Makes sense. What will become of this place?'

'It's going to be turned into a hotel. Houses will be

built on the golf course. Arrow Lake is a very up-and-coming resort, all year round.'

'Not like the heyday of the Catskills though,' Dani said. 'Years ago, there were so many resorts, but now there are practically none.'

'And that's where we come in. This town has gone through a resurgence over the past few years and we want to make sure it gets better and better. World class hotels, top notch facilities. This summer, we're bringing that to the region. The new club will also be a five-star hotel and resort, and the houses in the grounds will be exclusive. We also have a world-famous golfer helping design the golf course.'

It was like Porter had slipped into sales pitch mode without realizing it.

'Do you think what's going on will affect your business?' I asked him.

'Not at all. Four years ago, we saw in increase in business after all that had gone on. Not to sound macabre, but Tom Morgan put this place on the map.'

'People came here after he died. They felt safe. Now we have somebody who is killing again and they're not in custody. It might be different this time around,' Dani said.

'We have the best security teams now. We're not taking any chances with guests' safety.' Porter didn't look so sure of himself.

'Mr Porter, make sure they're on the ball, especially over at the new building site. Make sure it's well-lit at night and have armed patrols going about. This man is dangerous.'

I didn't want to let on that we thought there were two men involved.

'I will. I'll give my men orders to let him have it if he comes on our property.' He looked at his watch. 'If you'll excuse me, I have work to catch up with.'

'Thank you for showing us around,' Dani said. 'I'll have a team come over today. If you could make sure nobody touches those machines.'

Porter assured us he would and we went our separate ways.

Dani's phone rang after we got back in the car, the cold air welcome. Atticus jumped over the back seat and greeted us like we'd been away for hours and I petted him while Dani pressed the button on her steering wheel to take the call.

'Detective Fox,' she said.

'It's Doctor Lazio over at the morgue.'

'Hello, doc. You're on speaker in my car.'

'I'm assuming Agent Marshall is there with you?'

'You assume correctly,' I told him.

'Good morning, too, Scott. I just wanted to let you know I have an ID on the woman who was hanging in the woods.' He paused for effect. 'It's one of our own victims; Angela Kerr.'

'There's no doubt?' I said to him.

'None whatsoever. We have all the dental records on file for the women who are still missing. We just matched Miss Kerr's.'

'Thanks,' Dani said. 'We'll go and find her next of kin now.' She ended the call. Looked at me. I was sweating despite the cold air inside the car. It wasn't Jessie. Maybe he'd display her later.

I could only hope.

TWELVE

Far Horizon's was just outside of town. It was a trailer park, but it was very well kept. It looked like it was a nice place to live if you were on a budget. Which Bruce Kerr obviously was.

His trailer was a double-wide. It had parking for two cars at the front and a little bit of lawn at the side and front.

There were some stairs leading up to the door which had a small deck in front of it.

'Seems like a nice place,' I said. The units on this row backed up to the woods, and there were trees in between each unit offering some shade.

'It is. We don't get many calls out to here. probably because it's for over fifty-fives.'

Dani knocked on the front door and a few minutes later it was answered.

I looked around at the car again just to make sure the engine was running so Atticus could stay cool.

Bruce Kerr was in his sixties. Balding. Weasel eyes. He viewed us with suspicion, peering at Dani's badge like she'd just made it herself before coming here.

'Thought you were one of them snoopin' reporters,' he said, closing the front door behind us. The house smelled of stale tobacco and coffee.

'You've had reporters here already?' I said.

'No. From the last time. I thought they were back, but I guess it's too early. Give them time, though.'

'I want to ask you a few questions about Angela, Mr Kerr,' Dani said.

'Sit down, both of you,' Kerr said, easing himself into a high-back chair, grimacing as he leaned back.

I moved a few old newspapers so we could sit down.

'I'm sorry, but we have some bad news,' Dani said.

'Angela's dead. Tell me something I don't know.'

His words took Dani by surprise for a moment but she quickly caught herself. 'She is, yes. She was missing for four years and somebody displayed her body in the woods last night.'

'I told that crowd they were a bunch of no-good sons of bitches.'

'Who are we talking about?' I asked.

'Chief Walker and his department. I told them

something funny was going on with Angela all those years ago. Nobody believed me though. Nobody came around and took a statement. Said she was a big girl and that if anything, I was wasting their time.' Kerr shook his head. 'My little girl was hurting and nobody took any notice. They said she was an adult and if she wanted to leave and not be found, that was her prerogative. It was only after a week and there was no activity on her bank account did they start to take it seriously.'

'Was there any activity on her cell phone?' I asked.

Dani looked at me. 'We checked the records and it was in the town the night she went missing, then nothing. It stopped pinging, like the battery was out or it had been switched off.'

'Not to mention her car was still here,' Kerr said. 'They even had an answer for that too; if people want to disappear, they leave everything behind and start a new life. I got right in Walker's face. To be honest though, he was a good guy. I just gave him a hard time. And you know what was the worst thing? Tom Morgan was right there, listening. The man who killed those women.'

I didn't contradict him. It wasn't the time. 'The night Angela disappeared, did she tell you where she was going?' I asked him.

'No, not that night. A week or so before, she said she was going to meet some guy on a blind date. The night she went missing, she said she needed to meet someone, but she wasn't dressed for a date or anything. Ellen was missing and she was worried. I never saw her again.'

'Did you tell Walker this?' Dani asked.

'I did at the time, but he didn't want to know.'

'Do you know anything at all about this blind date?' I asked him. 'Any specific details about the man she was meeting?'

The old man shook his head, as if all the anger had expelled itself from him. 'Nothing. Nothing at all. She'd got divorced, he'd moved away to Buffalo and she had moved in with me after the house was sold. She was looking for a new place.'

I turned to Dani. 'Was the husband checked out?'

'Yes. He had a rock-solid alibi. He wasn't anywhere near here at the time Angela went missing.'

'She was a nurse, wasn't she?' I recalled that fact from reading through the case notes again.

'Yes. I suppose she came into contact with Tom Morgan through her job. She came into contact with a lot of weirdos that way. This town's population pales when you take into account the number of visitors we get.'

'What type of nurse was she? What department?'

'She was an ER nurse.'

'Did she go out much? Socializing?' I asked Kerr.

'Not that I remember. She probably did, but most of the time, she was exhausted after work. She didn't have time for dating. So, she thought this blind date thing was a good idea.'

'Who introduced her to this blind date?'

Kerr looked like he had lost focus for a moment, but he was just searching his memory bank. 'She kept insisting that it wasn't a blind date, but I've been round the block a few times. She said she had met him in one of those chat rooms. He was a local guy, apparently, but she hadn't seen a photo of him. She was meeting him in a bar. I suggested that she meet in a place that had a lot of people in it. She was excited about it. I suggested she tell somebody where she was going and she told me one of her friends said she would go too but sit somewhere else. Keep an eye on Angela.'

'Did she tell you his name?' I was appalled that this information had been given to the police back in the day, but I had never heard this story before. Not when I came with the original team, nor a year later. I looked at Dani who looked just as shocked as I did.

'No. He never turned up. She said some of the workers from the hospital turned up and they had a few drinks and it was a good night, despite Romeo not making an appearance.'

'Who was the friend?' I asked again.

'One of the nurses she worked with.'

'I don't suppose you remember who it was?' I said, not feeling much hope.

'Of course I do. It was her one friend. The girl who she went through nursing school with; Ellen Wood. One of the other victims. After that night, Angela never heard from the guy on the internet again, and it was around a week later, Ellen went missing. My daughter wanted to talk to somebody about that, but she didn't trust Tom Morgan. Morgan had asked her out a few times, despite him being married. Angela thought he was a creep, so she didn't trust any of the detectives.' He looked at Dani. 'No offense.'

'None taken.'

'That's why she got in touch with you lot. The feds.'

I looked puzzled. 'Do you know who she spoke to?'

'I don't know if she actually spoke to the agent, because that was the night she disappeared. The agent's name was Jessie Kent.'

Outside, I was shivering despite the heat. I had the tailgate open on the Tahoe after asking for Dani's keys. I sat in the cargo area and hugged Atticus. I told myself that he was needing to be reassured, but I was lying to myself.

I watched as Dani thanked Kerr at his front door. My FBI partner, Jessie Kent, had left the hotel that night to meet Angela Kerr.

'You okay?' Dani asked me as she came round to the back of the car. Atticus wagged his tail off and licked her face as she rubbed either side of his face.

'Of course I am. I'm an ex-federal agent. I'm trained not to show my emotions in front of anybody.' I looked at her. 'If that's the case, why are my eyes stinging?'

'You're human. You miss her, don't you? Jessie.'

'She was the best partner I ever had. She saved my life on more than one occasion, but the one that sticks in my head more than any is the time we were hunting a murderer who was killing women with an ax. We were closing in on him. The team split up, going to two locations. We were convinced he was at one of them. Ours was an old house. It had been abandoned but it had been in his family years before.

'Anyway, we went in and I was searching upstairs, and I thought I'd cleared a room, but there was a hidden room behind a closet wall. He came out and swung the ax at me. My instinct made me jump out of the way and he missed but before I could get a shot off, he back-handed me and I fell to the floor, my gun spinning away. He took the ax out of the wall and took it two-handed and swung it back behind his head to bring it down on me. Jessie emptied her clip into him.'

'Oh my God, Scott.' She rubbed my arm.

'I miss her, Dani, but every day I realize just how much I let her down. She was there for me, but I wasn't there for her. I need to find who took her.'

'We won't stop looking.'

I took a couple of minutes to compose myself. I very rarely let my guard down and showed my emotions but hearing that the woman I once thought of as my best friend had been going to meet this woman, who herself became a victim, made it feel like ice was running through my veins.

'Let's think about this,' I said to her. 'Angela and Ellen are in the pub, Angela to meet a stranger she met online. Ellen is there watching. The guy doesn't turn up, but it's no big loss because friends of theirs turn up. A week or so later, Ellen goes missing. Angela seems to know something and arranges to talk to Jessie, and that night, they both go missing.'

'That sounds about right.'

'I think Angela saw the killer the night she was supposed to meet the guy she'd met online.'

'You think *he* was the killer?'

'I do. But I think he got Angela to go there so he could observe her. He was there that night, watching her in plain sight. I think she figured it out a few days later when Ellen went missing and she was going to confide in the one person she trusted; Jessie.'

'We can look at witness statements, from the people who were in the pub that night. See if anything jumps out at us.'

'I'm assuming that the names would have been put through the database?'

'They would have. But let us look at the names with a fresh pair of eyes.'

We closed the tailgate and got back in the car. It was strange, but I felt we were getting closer to finding our killer.

And to finding Jessie.

THIRTEEN

Zach Porter flopped down on his couch and slipped his shoes off.

'Hard day?' his wife asked. She smiled and handed him a can of Coors Light.

'Just the usual.' He popped the tab and drank from it, chugging it back His wife scuttled away for another one, knowing this one would be empty by the time she got back.

He burped loudly, crushed the can and tossed it into the trash can next to him. It had been emptied earlier in the day. Unlike yesterday. She had forgotten. Again. She hadn't forgotten today.

She knew better.

'Dinner won't be long,' she said, handing him the next can.

'It better not be burnt again.'

'It isn't. I'm more careful now.'

'We've been married for years. You would think you knew how to cook by now.'

'Some women go their whole lives without learning how to cook.'

'They wouldn't be married to me if they didn't.'

She ignored the last remark and handed him the TV remote. He switched it on. It wasn't one of those big monster TVs that people seemed to fawn over nowadays. He didn't want one of those. Not after he read how the big companies used them to spy on people. There were even some refrigerators that had TV screens in them. Once again, he had read about those hackers who tapped into them, stealing computing power, or some such thing. Nope, you were better off with an old TV and a good old Frigidaire. You could watch football on one and keep your beer cold in the other. What more did a man want?

'What are the girls doing?'

'They're both in bed, of course.'

Zach thought she was going to add the word *obviously* at the end of her sentence, but she knew better. After the last time.

'I thought Zoe would have stayed up to see her daddy. You know, the person who brings in the bacon.'

'She's three, Zach. Daphne's eighteen months. They need their sleep. Maybe one day a week you could make a point of coming home a bit earlier.'

'You did hear me say I brought the bacon home, didn't you?'

'Yes.'

'I have to work hard. My father isn't going to give me handouts now, is he?'

'You could always ask.'

Zach screwed his face up. 'He thinks he gives me enough as it is. The last thing I want is to go begging to him.' He gulped down the rest of his can.

'You want another one before you eat?' she asked him.

'No. I have to go back to work later.' He yawned. 'I don't want to get pulled over. But you'd like that, wouldn't you?'

'Don't say that.' She wrung her hands together. 'I'll go and serve dinner.'

'Yes, go and do that. I want to eat then have a nap before I go out.' He flipped through the channels before settling on *Jeopardy!* This was his favorite show. One of the staples of regular TV. The rest didn't grab him much, so he had been binging on Netflix recently.

He and his wife slept not only in separate beds, but separate rooms. It suited him fine. He often lay in bed watching a show on his iPad. His smaller TV had given up the ghost a long time ago and he didn't want one of the spying machines. His iPad was just fine. He put a bit tape over the camera lens.

His wife didn't have access to the wi-fi. He could only imagine how little housework would get done if she could watch TV all day.

'Dinner's ready,' she said, coming back into the living room. He got up, feeling tired from a hard day's work, but also feeling a buzz of excitement.

He had to admit the food smelled good. Ziti. With little bits of sausages thrown in, just how he liked it.

They sat at the dining table and made small talk. They would discuss the things she had watched on the news. That was one thing he did insist she do. That way they would have something to discuss when he got home. Otherwise, there would be nothing.

Afterwards, she cleared away the table. 'I'm going upstairs for a nap,' he told her. She merely nodded. There was a book she wanted to start reading.

Three hours later, he got up, showered and dressed in casual clothes. Ones that hadn't been worn yet and would never be worn again.

He stood in the middle of his garage, looking down at the plastic-wrapped corpse. He was picturing her in his mind; there was a certain beauty to her face. She had a slightly round nose, but her eyes were her best feature. Brown. They had stared at him as she pleaded for her life. She had died relatively quickly. Only because she wasn't part of the original plan.

The side door to the garage opened and another figure stepped in. 'You're late,' Zach said.

'So sue me. Oh, wait...'

Zach shook his head. 'Just get in here and close the door.'

'We still carrying out the plan we went over before?'

'No, I thought we could take her dancing first.' Zach looked at his friend.

'Boy, are you in a mood tonight. What happened? Wife burn the dinner again?'

'You would think so, but it was decent for a change.' He opened the driver's door of the Wrangler. 'Let's get this done. I don't want to still be there when she gets back. That would be an unfortunate event.'

'It certainly would be an added complication,' his friend said.

They put her in the back of his Jeep and closed the door.

'I wish we could have spent more time together in this life,' he said as the garage door rolled up. 'Sadly, it wasn't meant to be. I do hope you're not offended.'

He got in behind the wheel and they drove out into the darkness.

FOURTEEN

Dani's mom and dad were babysitting Atticus for a few hours.

'It's nice to have a man in the house again,' she said to me. 'Even if it's just going to be for a little while.'

'I have to admit, it's nice having company. Maria, my housekeeper, likes to catch up on her shows at night. Sometimes, I'll treat her to dinner out, but she's off the clock in the evening. It's usually just me and Atticus.'

We got in her Tahoe and she waved to her mom. Atticus was inside with Bill, probably demanding that his ball be thrown for him.

'I thought you would have been out wooing the women of Newburgh,' she said with a smile.

'I've had my moments. How's the singles scene up here?'

'Surprisingly, not too shabby. We have a singles night in one of the nightclubs, plus the nightclubs themselves and there are quite a few bars. But if you're asking if I frequent them, then no. Having a cop dancing the night away would spoil the vibe.'

'What *do* you do for fun?'

'I don't have time for fun. Except when I'm with you,' she said with a grin.

She hit the main road and we headed round to the country club. Where we were going to meet up with Nikki Hunter. The town's big wig Magnus Porter was holding a conference, reassuring potential buyers and investors that they were safe.

We were shown into the large lounge again. Raif Porter was there. He came over to us when he recognized Dani.

'Detective Fox! Good to see you again.' He looked at me and his smile didn't miss a beat. 'Who's your friend?'

I thought it a strange question since he already knew me, then the answer came to me.

'Scott Marshall, this is Finn Porter.' She looked at me. 'Raif you met, so I figured that if he didn't know you, then it must be Finn.'

'Good to meet you, Scott.' He shook hands with me.

'Likewise.'

'Where's your brother?' Dani asked him.

'Skulking about somewhere. Trying to persuade people not to pull their money out, but to be honest, all this mention of a killer puts us on the map. You would think that it would put people off buying a house in the new country club, but phase one was sold out after the last debacle here. Phase two was just sold out last week and we've already had deposits put on phase three.'

I looked over to where Porter Senior was standing. He was laughing with some men, presumably his cronies. I saw Chief Hunter standing talking to somebody else. She didn't look as intimidating without her Chief's uniform on though the gun on her hip might deter anyone who thought she was an easy mark.

The room was filled with people dressed as if they were coming to a cocktail party. I heard Porter's voice cutting through the babble and everybody turned their attention to him. He had stepped up on the stage where the resident band played at the weekends. A podium had been set up and his deep voice assaulted us through the loudspeakers.

'Ladies and gentlemen, I have the pleasure of introducing our town's Chief of Police, Nikki Hunter. I've asked her to come here tonight to speak with you.' He turned to Nikki. 'Chief, if you wouldn't mind?'

He gave her a round of applause like she was the next act in a comedy routine.

Nikki hid her embarrassment well as she stepped up onto the stage. I wondered if she felt tempted to draw her firearm and let him have it.

'Thank you, Mr Porter. Ladies and gentlemen, I was asked to come here and reassure you that there is nothing to worry about in our town. Yes, we have a small problem, but the matter is being investigated.'

'A problem?' one man shouted from the crowd. He was obviously well on his way to becoming very drunk and was at the stage where voicing an opinion wasn't being held back by rationale but rather encouraged by copious amounts of alcohol. 'Having a serial killer running about the town is hardly trying to find a repeat jaywalker!'

Nikki kept calm and addressed the man directly. 'The town is still a safe place to be, sir. There's nothing for anybody to worry about.'

'Unless you wake up to find a dead woman hanging from a tree in your backyard.'

I saw Magnus Porter indicating with his head to his son. Finn gritted his teeth and indicated in turn to some security men to go over and apprehend the drunk. Three very large men walked over and grabbed the man by the elbows and guided him out after taking his glass from him.

'That's it! Silence the little man! But I won't be silenced, Porter!'

Finn came back over as the security men took him outside. 'My apologies. He's a regular here but he's known to have one too many. I'll see to it that he's barred for life now.'

'He might have a point,' I said, sipping the glass of seltzer I had been given.

'What do you mean?' Finn Porter's demeanor changed in a heartbeat.

'When a killer strikes in a town, it puts fear into people. That's a fact. People who would not normally lock their door start to. Kids are escorted to the school bus. Women go for a night out in pairs and go home in pairs or small groups. It can strike at the heart of any town.'

'Well, hopefully you'll catch him before he does too much damage. How long did it take four years ago? Six weeks?'

'He was active for almost three weeks before we caught him,' Dani said.

'Oh yes, I forgot; he was one of yours.' He looked at Dani, waiting for her to argue. She didn't.

'We'll do everything in our power to catch him,' I said, keeping my voice low as Nikki started her talk again.

Finn nodded. 'I know. I'm sorry. It's getting to everybody. I heard about somebody shooting at you.

Well, I for one will be glad when that damn park is finally closed.'

Dani looked puzzled. 'What do you mean, *closed*?'

'That's part of the new development. From the new club right round to where the park is.'

'You're closing a park?' I said to him. 'Surely the public won't be happy about that?'

'It's our land. My grandfather let the town use it until one such day when we wanted it back. That day is now. There are more parks and trails.'

'People are going to miss it,' Dani said.

'It is what it is. It's hard staying afloat in today's world,' Finn said, looking past me towards the front door to make sure the drunk had been taken out. I had expected him to say, *No pun intended* but he didn't.

'Excuse me,' he said, walking away.

'You didn't tell me Raif had a twin brother,' I said to Dani.

'You didn't ask.' There was a slight grin on her face. 'Sorry. I forgot to mention it. I thought you knew from four years ago.'

'I never met the brothers,' I told her.

'Really? You met Magnus Porter though, right?'

'I saw him. Chief Walker was dealing with him, and I think one of my team met with him, but I never did.'

'I thought you had. Anyway, he has twin sons and a daughter.'

'How old is the daughter?' I asked.

'Twenty-two. Raif and Finn are twenty-five.'

'They seem like a decent pair of guys.'

'They're already working for their father. They were guaranteed a job after coming home from college.'

'It's always the way.' I looked around. Porter was talking and laughing with a group of what appeared to be businessmen.

Nikki Hunter walked over to us. 'Next time, I'll chew my arm off rather than come here and speak. I know it's my job to reassure the public, but these people are hardly John Q Public. Rich boys and girls who want to know their money is going to be well looked after. My job is to protect and serve the citizens of this town.'

'Still no sign of a murder victim?' I asked her.

'You would be the first to know, Scott,' she said.

They still hadn't found the person who the blood on the shroud belonged to.

All that was about to change.

FIFTEEN

'That's what people get for living out in a place where they can't see the neighbors for the trees,' Zach Porter said. 'People like us can do whatever we like to their house.'

He switched the headlights off, keeping the side-lights on, then switched them off when they pulled up to the double garage. He pulled his mask down, put gloves on, and took the hammer out and smashed the double spotlight that had come on above the garage doors. The driveway was thrown into darkness again.

The light had also come on above the front door but a racoon could have switched that on. Luckily for them, this wasn't a main road. It wouldn't have made the job impossible, just a bit more difficult.

He took out the wire coat hanger, slipped it between the frame of one of the garage doors and the rubber seal, and managed to hook the manual release bar inside, which was there in case the power went so the occupant could still open the door.

He walked quickly back to the car, got his friend to help him carry the corpse out of the car, shut the car door and then they were in the garage, closing that door behind them.

They unwrapped the plastic from her, Zach having checked his friend also had gloves on. The form was stiff in the plastic but she was easy to carry.

Zach carried the top half, his friend taking the legs. He opened the door that led into the house. He knew where he was going. He'd been here before, not so long ago.

They didn't put any lights on but carried the corpse upstairs.

Ten minutes later, they were done and heading back out.

'Good job,' Zach said. His friend smiled.

'It was, wasn't it?'

They got in the Jeep and drove away.

***

Nikki Hunter got in her patrol SUV and drove away from the country club feeling disgusted. Magnus Porter had asked her to come along and give the talk and she had felt a sense of duty to go along. More people investing in the houses and the new club meant more investment for the town, and that was her main concern.

She had debated whether to go or not, considering that she wasn't going to be spending the rest of her life here. She wanted more than anything to catch her father's killer, then move on, but the question had buzzed around in her head for the longest time; what if you don't catch him?

It had been six months since her father had died and still nothing. Having Scott Marshall here helped bolster her confidence, but she had to face the reality that they might never be able to track the killer down. The town had thought that Tom Morgan was *The Gravedigger* but she and Marshall thought otherwise. Who the hell could it be? And why did he have a four-year hiatus?

Her head was spinning by the time she pulled into her road. The headlights cut through the darkness. She'd always known she wanted to get out of this town one day, and achieving that had made her feel good. Now she was back, it felt like she had stepped back in time.

She liked Scott Marshall. When Dani Fox had suggested they bring him back in, she had balked at the idea, but had decided to give him a chance. Now she was glad he was here.

She pulled the Tahoe into her driveway, stopping in front of the double garage doors. The lights above them didn't come on. She was wary when she stepped out onto the concrete apron. She took out her flashlight and put her hand on her gun.

Broken glass twinkled at her from the ground. She shone the flashlight up at the lights. Then the adrenaline kicked in as she saw they were smashed.

What now? Call for back-up or go into the house? What would she say to the despatcher? Somebody smashed my security lights and now I'm scared to go into the house alone?

No, this had to be done. Besides, she'd been trained and was armed.

She let herself into the house, pointing her gun in front of her.

She carried on through each room, shining her flashlight, her senses on high alert. Downstairs was empty. She wanted to check upstairs before going down to the basement.

First the bathroom. Clear. Then her master bedroom.

She took a deep breath and swung the light into the room. And froze.

SIXTEEN

Dani's house had central air con and it was good to get out of the sticky humidity that even Arrow Lake couldn't subdue.

'Do you still drink?' she asked me. I was automatically looking around, waiting for Atticus to come bounding along the hall, wanting me to play ball with him, until I remembered he was over at Bill's.

'I have the odd beer. Not as much as I used to.' I didn't want to tell her I didn't drink at all nowadays. I never wanted to let my guard down again. I would rather stay stone cold sober and be able to defend myself, than be lying in a stupor, waiting for somebody to deliver the fatal blow.

'I have a few cold beers in the refrigerator, if you want one?'

'You go ahead if you want. I'm fine.'

She stepped up to me and smiled. 'You don't drink at all, do you?'

'Is it that obvious?'

'Not too much, but here I am, a beautiful blonde you're home alone with me, there's beer and you're refusing one. Most guys would jump at the chance to have a beer with me.'

'And you're modest with it, too. I like that in a woman. But here I am, a handsome young man, alone with a beautiful blonde and not having a drink with her. What does that say about me?'

'That you're a gentleman?' She laughed. 'It's okay if you prefer not to have sex.'

I held up my hands. 'I do like sex, but I don't turn into a slobbering monster in the company of a beautiful woman.'

She took me by the hand and led me upstairs. Into her room.

'I've thought about our night in my dad's cabin many times since that night three years ago. I don't regret it for one moment. And when I told you I haven't been out with many men, I meant that too. I was just waiting for that one man to walk into my life, and I think he just did. Again.'

She kissed me hard and started ripping at my shirt.

'It's been a long time for me,' I told her. 'There haven't been any women in my life since... you. It took me a long time to heal, mentally, and I don't think I'm quite there yet.'

'I promise I'll be gentle,' she said, and I could tell she didn't mean it.

I hesitated but then I cleared my mind. This wasn't wrong. We were two consenting adults. I wasn't taking advantage of her but all the justifications in the world didn't stop me from feeling just a little bit of guilt. I tried to keep the image of Jessie Kent out of my mind. It mostly worked.

I saw her smiling face, the last time I'd seen her.

Then I let Dani take over and it was the sweetest love making I'd ever had.

I lay under her sheet afterwards, sweating. Out of breath like I'd just started training for a marathon, but this was only the warm up. Tonight wasn't going to be a marathon. This was the five K fun run.

'Aren't you going to tell me you love me?' Dani said, looking over at me, lying by my side.

'Oh. Yes, of course; I love you.'

She laughed and playfully slapped my shoulder. 'I'm kidding, silly.' She was catching her own breath. 'I do have feelings for you, Scott. I'm not going to lie. But I don't want you to run out and buy me a ring tomorrow. I would like to see more of you, if you want. When this is over.'

I couldn't think of a better idea. 'I'd like that.' I

leaned over and kissed her gently on the lips. And I meant it. Had I subconsciously not made a go of it with other women because Dani was in the back of my mind? No, I didn't think so. Maybe a psychologist would be able to figure it out. Right now, I was happy and so was Dani. This was today. Tomorrow was never promised.

'Can I ask you something?' I said.

'Of course. Ask me anything you want. I can't promise I'll answer, but I'll certainly give it some thought.' She gave a small laugh. It was the same one I remembered from the last time we had spent the night together. Back when I was drinking to blot out the sun. Before eight-week-old Atticus came into my life.

'Why did you come back to live here? I know you went through the divorce, but why not stay in New York?'

The smile slipped for a moment, and I could see something in her eyes, something locked away and no key was going to unlock it. Not tonight, maybe not ever.

'Sorry, that's none of my business, 'I said.

She laid a hand on my chest. 'I'll tell you. One day. Just not tonight.' She laid her head against my chest and I could feel the tears on my skin.

I thought that maybe she was crying for a marriage that had been hard won but easily lost.

I was wrong.

I gently stroked her hair, mentally kicking myself for asking such a personal question. *Too soon, Scott.* I thought about telling her I didn't mean to pry but decided she was best left alone with her thoughts. I felt her breath slowing down, as if she was so comfortable with me, she could fall asleep on me, which made me feel good. I wanted her to trust me, which I felt she did, and I trusted her with my life.

I felt myself starting to slip into a comfortable slumber when my cell phone rang. I went from nearly falling asleep to fully awake in a heartbeat. Like when Atticus started barking and ran to the front door and I got up to find nothing there.

Dani moved away from me as I reached over to the nightstand on my side of the bed and picked up my phone.

'*Scott? It's her. She's here in my house. He put her here, in my house.*'

Nikki Hunter kept talking but I was already up and getting dressed.

SEVENTEEN

It seemed like the whole of the police department was at Nikki Hunter's house. She was standing outside, two of her other detectives standing close by.

I parked Dani's Tahoe in the street and we walked over to her. She excused herself and stood looking at me.

'Thank you for coming. Both of you.'

'What's wrong, Nicky?' I asked her.

'The killer was in my house.'

'How do you know?' Dani asked.

'Let me show you.'

We walked through the crowd of forensics officers, patrol officers, and a bunch of other people who were normally called out to a crime scene of this nature.

She took us inside. Every light was on in the house.

'It's been photographed and videoed. She's still up here.'

We followed her upstairs to her bedroom where the naked corpse was sprawled out on her bed. Her throat had been cut, which would explain the blood on the shroud that Angela Kerr had been wearing, if this woman had been wearing it first.

'It's Cathy Kerr.' I stood looking down at the woman who we had spoken to not long ago. I had told her to be safe, but now I felt I should have done more for her. I hadn't thought she would be in danger. I was wrong.

I was looking down at the young woman, at her sightless eyes and the wide rent in her throat.

'Do you think she was picked at random or singled out because of Angela?' Dani asked me.

I turned to look at her. 'Definitely because of Angela.'

We heard commotion behind us and Lou Fazio, the medical examiner, came in with one of his assistants.

'Good to see you again, Scott. Chief. Dani.' He put his bag down and pulled on a pair of gloves. He stood looking at the girl.

'Come on then, Cathy, let's get you seen to,' he said.

'You know her, then?' I asked him.

He turned to me. 'She works at the hospital. She's a nurse. I've seen her around.'

We went back downstairs to leave the medical professionals to do their thing.

Outside, the night was much cooler with a sharp wind adding to the falling temperatures. Nikki Hunter came out, followed by one of her senior detectives.

'Somebody's either trying to frighten me or frame me,' she said.

'It's hard on everybody,' Dani said. 'Especially people like Lou, who knew the victim.'

'I agree. It just seems that our killer can do whatever he likes, whenever he likes.'

'At least we know she wasn't killed in your house,' I said. 'Lack of blood.'

'That's one saving grace. So we'll work on the theory he's trying to scare me off the case. I hope he's not holding his breath.'

'Do you have anywhere to stay tonight?' I asked her.

'My dad's old place. I'm in the middle of doing it up so I can stay in it until it gets sold. It's more work than I envisioned.'

'I know. My house needed gutting when I moved in. It takes time.'

'Will you be okay on your own?' Dani asked her.

'I'll be fine. He's wanting to send me a message now, too. Trying to scare me off.'

I nodded as if agreeing, but something told me that this went far deeper.

Dani and I stayed for a while, waiting until the body was taken out of the house in a body bag.

'Looks like the cause of death was the knife wound in her neck,' Fazio said.

'Or a sharp instrument,' I said, thinking that the man wasn't quite as professional as Dani's father had been, when he was the medical examiner.

We were almost home at Dani's when her phone rang. She spoke into it then hung up.

'That was my-ex. He just got back from honeymoon. He's starting back at work tomorrow and he'll look into the Sofia Martinez case for us.'

'I think I should go down there. Talk to him and have a word with the family.'

'If that's what you want. I can call him and let him know.'

I was sure Atticus would be okay with Dani and her dad.

She made the call.

EIGHTEEN

Bill was delighted to be having Atticus stay with them for a little while. Not so delighted when he found I was going down to New York City to meet up with Dani's ex.

'Dad, don't worry,' she had explained to him the night before. 'Eddie's got a new wife now. They were just on honeymoon.'

'I hope the new woman in his life went into the marriage with eyes wide open.'

'For goodness sake.'

I sat opposite Bill at their kitchen table. 'The first victim that was found came from the Bronx. He's agreed to help us, Bill, and if that means us getting closer to the killer up here, then I'm willing to go with it. For the woman's family's sake.'

'I suppose you're right.' He drank some more of his

hot chocolate. 'This is getting on my nerves. I'm glad Lou Fazio is in charge now. I bet he didn't know what he was letting himself in for when he came here.'

I got the impression that Bill didn't like the idea that Lou Fazio could take a serial killer in his stride, but like all people about to retire, he thought he was indispensable. He had been there for Lou Fazio's transition period, even though he didn't need to be. Just to show the new guy the ropes, he had said.

'Lou worked down in the Bronx, Dad,' Dani said. 'I'm sure he had his fair share of murders to deal with.'

'Oh jeez!' Sylvia shouted, scooting her chair back as the mug of coffee dropped from her hand onto the table. We stood up as the hot liquid spread across the table like a tsunami and Dani ran to grab a towel.

'I'm so sorry,' Sylvia said. 'What a klutz.'

'Don't worry,' I said to her. 'We'll just make fun of you next time we see you.'

She laughed and slapped my arm.

Dani and I left Bill and Sylvia, promising to return in the morning with Atticus.

'I really need to get one of those security systems where you can check the inside of your house on the phone before you go inside.'

She opened the door and I stood with Atticus, letting him sniff the air. He didn't seem to detect anything out of the ordinary. I slipped his leash and let him run into the house. There were no notes, no bodies lying in the backyard.

'I'm going to have a glass of wine. Would you like anything?' Dani asked me.

'I'm going to hit the hay. We're up early tomorrow. If you're still up for driving me down to Albany airport?'

'Of course I am. My mum and dad don't go to bed late and they get up early. We can drop Atticus off before I take you.'

The dog stood looking at Dani, his head tilted to one side, like he knew we were talking about him.

'You're okay, boy,' I said to him and he ran off to fetch one of his balls and brought it back for me to throw to him.

'Go ahead,' Dani said, 'I don't have any Ming vases.'

I smiled and threw the ball down the hall. Atticus liked to play for five minutes before bed. Sometimes at home he would play by himself, which consisted of him throwing his bed around the living room or running up and down the hall, skidding to a halt at the front door, scrunching up the rug.

'You know, I think I'll skip the wine. I'm feeling a bit tired. But not too tired.' She took me by the hand and led me upstairs.

NINETEEN

The next morning was sunny and warm. It almost felt like I was going on vacation. I had a bag packed for an overnight stay, and I was being driven to the airport by a friend. Or was she becoming more than a friend? The previous night would suggest so.

'I'll call the Chief before I go to work,' Dani said. 'See how she's doing.'

'I think she would have called us if anything else transpired.'

'She was staying at her father's cabin. It must be nerve-wracking.'

'I know.' The traffic was heavy in parts as we headed down I87. Dani looked good, and it almost felt like I was leaving my wife behind to go on a trip. But I gave myself a reality check when I thought about Eddie

Flint, who really had been her husband. What was I, in her big scheme of things?

It was morning rush hour but we made good time. Two and a half hours after leaving Arrow Lake, Dani was dropping me off for my flight down to New York.

'You sure you don't want me to come in and wait with you?' she asked.

I smiled. 'I'll be fine. I'd rather you get home.' I kissed her goodbye and made my way to the ticket desk and then went through to security to wait for my flight to be called. Less than an hour later, we were in the air.

The flight took less time than the drive down, and I was off the plane and into my rental car in no time.

I knew my way around Manhattan, but only to a certain level. It had been a while since I had driven there, but nothing had changed. It still took me over an hour to get to Eddie Flint's 24th Precinct on the Upper West Side on W 82nd. I parked in a parking garage across the road and walked the short distance to what looked like a small office building sitting right next door to a firehouse. Cruisers and three-wheeler parking vehicles sat outside.

A female uniform took me upstairs to where Eddie Flint was waiting.

'Detective Flint, Scott Marshall to see you.' She left and I found myself doing a quick profile of the man as we shook hands; he was around thirty, worked out, took care of his appearance, and loved himself. We sat down at his desk.

'I believe you're just back from honeymoon,' I said. 'Somewhere warm?'

'Aruba. My wife always wanted to go, so I took her there on honeymoon. Killed two birds with one stone. Saved my wallet a whole bunch of money.' He grinned.

A layman might have thought I was making small talk but I'd mentioned the honeymoon to lay down the foundation that I knew he had been married to Dani and now he'd moved on.

'I hear you. It doesn't do any harm to save a few bucks.'

He was eying me up, wondering if there was some angle I was working but he couldn't seem to think of anything so he absentmindedly picked up a pencil and started tapping it on the desk.

'Dani told me about the trouble she's having back up in Arrow Lake. I thought that was done and dusted four years ago.'

'You and me both.'

'You got shot five times and lived?' He said it like he was impressed.

'I'm here to tell the tale, but only because of the paramedics and the surgeons who saved my life.'

'Those people are the business. But tell me more about the case you're working on.'

I outlined what was going on and how it was related to the case from four years ago.

He nodded. 'Right. I've done a little background on the misper. She lived and worked in the Bronx, but she disappeared after going to a club down in the Bowery. Friends saw her get into a car with a man but they were all jacked up on drink and whatever else they shove up their noses. Nobody really saw anything. We can go and talk to her parents again. They've already been given the death notice and no doubt the press will be digging it all up again.'

A woman came up behind us. 'It's already all over social media. Everybody has an opinion, especially the trolls.'

I looked round at her. She was holding a cup of something. Maybe ice tea.

'Scott, this is Dawn Helmsley. My partner.'

I made to stand up, pushing on the edge of his desk. Pain shot through my knee.

'Don't get up,' she said, as I was straightening up.

Dawn was big, built heavier than Eddie, wearing a suit that was too tight. She had short hair and dark, hooded eyes.

She held out a hand for me to shake. I gripped and she started to tighten her hand so I stuck my index and middle fingers along her wrist, a trick I'd learned a long time ago. Now she could squeeze as hard as she liked but couldn't crush my hand. She gave up and let go. I resisted the temptation to wipe my hand on my pants.

'He didn't just shoot me five times, he kicked my knee out,' I said to Eddie.

'Plays up in bad weather, huh?' he said. I nodded.

'It's nice outside,' Dawn said. Meaning, *What's your excuse when it's sunny?* Anybody who's had a partial knee dislocation would know.

'I sat in a car for two and half hours, a plane for almost two hours, then I drove here from Newark, almost two hours. I'm a bit stiff.'

She took a sip of her drink through the straw and gave Eddie a look which she thought I wouldn't decipher, but when you look and smirk, a schoolboy can tell what you mean.

'Right, I'll let you hold the fort, Dawn, while Scott and I drive up to see Sofia's parents. They're expecting us.'

'By *hold the fort*, do you mean, catch up with our paperwork?' she asked, her brow furrowing.

'I mean, do whatever makes you happy.' He grabbed his suit jacket and we headed out of the squad room and downstairs, out into the early afternoon sunshine.

'Dawn's a good partner but she's just a bit...'

'Intense?' I suggested.

'Yeah, let's go with that.'

It had been a while since I was in Manhattan. I thought back to the previous year when my folks had come up from Florida and I'd taken my father to the Jacob Javits Center for the auto show. We'd spent a few hours sitting in cars that neither of us could afford, but we'd dreamt about winning the lottery and filling a garage with some.

I missed my father, and once again, I promised myself I would go and see them soon. I looked at the man getting in behind the wheel of the Crown Vic and wondered if he'd mind if I asked his ex-wife to come to Florida with me.

'I'll take my rental and follow you. I need to head to Westchester after this.'

'Sure thing.'

He waited and then we cut across Central Park to the East Side, up 1st Avenue and caught I278 then I95. The trip took just over half an hour.

We managed to park close to the house but still had to walk. The house was detached, a white, two-story with bars on the first-floor windows and on the door.

A man answered the door only after Eddie held up his badge. We were shown into a living room that was kept clean. A woman sat on the couch, holding a Kleenex which she used to rub at her nose.

'Thank you for seeing me,' I said. 'I'm ex-FBI and am consulting with the Arrow Lake PD.'

'This is such terrible news,' Mr Martinez said, sitting next to his wife. 'We were hoping that one day Sofia would walk back through the door. It's not going to happen now.'

'We need to catch the person who found your daughter and displayed her body,' I said. 'He's just as sick as her killer.'

Martinez looked at me. 'We still had hope, even after four years. Hope that she would return, no questions asked. But then we get a visit from a detective saying she'll never come back through the door.'

'That's why we need all the help we can get to find her killer and the person who found her.'

Mrs Martinez took the Kleenex away from her face. 'We told the police at the time. Sofia did. About the man. They didn't do nothing.'

'What man?' Eddie asked.

The mother looked at him. 'We told the police that Sofia had a stalker. Nobody was interested. Then she went missing. Then we tell them again, but still nothing.'

'Tell me about the stalker,' I told her. She switched her gaze from Eddie to me.

'It was at work. Little notes would be posted to her. Flowers would be delivered, always paid in cash and nobody knew nothing. Then she said she would see a car parked at night, somebody sitting in it, watching her. She couldn't be sure of course. One night, she went storming over to the driver, but it turned out to be somebody waiting for a girl. After that, she saw somebody sitting in a car, but she didn't approach. Then the letters arrived. And she got the feeling that she was being watched at work all the time.'

'She was a nurse, correct?' Eddie said.

'Yes, at the hospital down the road. Mercy University.'

'Did she report her suspicions to security?' I asked.

The woman shook her head. 'No. After a little while, it stopped. She figured he'd moved on to another victim. She didn't see anybody sitting in a car anymore. She told me she was relieved, but she was always wary. A few days later, she went missing.'

'Did she give any indication of who she thought it might be at the hospital?' Eddie asked.

'No,' Martinez replied. 'Or else I would have gone down and had a word with him.'

'Do you still have any of the notes or letters?' I asked the mother. She looked at her husband and nodded. He stood up and went over to a dresser. He opened a drawer and took out an envelope.

'The police didn't want to fingerprint it. I guess they were too busy dealing with *real* crimes,' he said, shooting Eddie a look.

I put on latex gloves, took the envelope, opened it

and took out a piece of paper. I read the three words written on it: *Alea iacta est*.

'It's Latin,' Martinez.

'The die is cast,' I translated.

'What do you think it means?' the mother asked.

After years of studying sociopaths and psychopaths, I knew exactly what it meant. 'Your daughter rejected this man, even though she hadn't met him and he took offense at this, so what he was going to do to her was set in stone. There was no going back.'

She began weeping again. My heart went out to her but there was nothing I could do to ease the pain, except find her daughter's killer.

'I'd like to take a photo of this if you don't mind?'

The woman nodded her permission. I took a photo with my phone. Eddie already had an evidence bag out and I put the note back into the envelope and then into the bag. 'The police will run this for fingerprints, but I'm assuming he was careful from what you've told me, and I don't think there will be anything there for them to lift.'

I let the mother get under control for a minute before speaking. 'The night your daughter went out to the nightclub, how did she get there?'

'She took a taxi to the subway station a few blocks away,' the mother answered.

'Did she go with anybody?'

'She was meeting her friends there.'

'And they were questioned after she went missing?' I said.

Eddie nodded. 'We took statements. A detective from the local precinct.'

'There is not one single day goes by we don't think about our daughter.'

'Did any of her friends tell you about the man she left with?'

Martinez cleared his throat. 'It was dark, the lights low, they were drinking. Nobody remembers much about much. It was a man. He hadn't been with her all night, but he was seen talking with her before she left.'

'Was your daughter drunk?' I asked.

Mrs Martinez's head shot up. 'No! Sofia didn't drink. And her friends confirmed she wasn't drinking that night.'

'So she was aware of her surroundings?'

'Of course.'

Mr Martinez spoke in a lower voice. 'They said, one minute she was there, the next, she was gone. She and the man she had been talking to.'

'And nothing seemed out of place? No arguments, anything like that?'

He shook his head. 'In fact, she had been laughing with him. She was relaxed in his company.'

I stood up then, sensing that I wouldn't get much more out of them. Eddie and I let ourselves out.

'What do you make of that?' he said.

The air was warm and thick with humidity. I pulled on a pair of sunglasses. Looked at Eddie.

'She knew her killer,' I said.

'How can you be so sure?'

'She didn't drink so she was sober. She was comfortable with him. When women have a drink, they let their guard down more. Sofia left with this man without any hesitation. She trusted him. After what she'd been through with getting the letters, she still felt safe leaving with him.'

'You think this other guy got to her somehow? The one who had sent her the letter?'

'No. I think it was one and the same person.'

I let him think about that for a moment. 'I'm going to see somebody else before I head north. I'm driving back. Thanks for coming with me.'

We shook hands. 'If you're ever down this way again, give me a call. Maybe we could catch a beer or something.'

'Will do. Stay safe, Eddie.'

I got in the car and put the directions into Google maps. My destination wasn't very far.

TWENTY

Trish Morgan lived in a decent-looking house in Mount Vernon, in Westchester County, north of where the Martinez family lived. I had called her beforehand and she was reluctant to see me at first, but I told her it was important.

She wore cargo shorts, a baggy t-shirt and Converse sneakers that had seen better days and looked like hand-me-downs. *Shabby chic*. I wondered if the expression applied here.

'Would you like something to drink?' she asked. I did, but I didn't want to accept anything from her. *Only drink something that's in a container that hasn't been opened, like a can of soda,* I'd been trained.

'No thanks,' I said, watching her walk away from the living room into the kitchen. Her hair was in need of a wash and cut, the dirty blonde looking straggly. I guessed life hadn't been kind to Trish Morgan. Trial by public opinion. It was never easy for the ones left behind, especially the ones who didn't know a loved one was a killer.

She came back in and sat down. Turned the speed down on the air conditioner, a unit that was old and cranky.

Trish was late thirties, touching forty. Her daughters were teenagers, one in middle school, the other a sophomore in high school.

'How's life treating you?' I asked her.

She shrugged, taking a cigarette from the packet lying on a small table next to her chair.

'Peachy. That's what I tell anybody who asks, somebody who doesn't know what it's like to have a serial killer for a husband.' She blew a plume of smoke out into a room that was already thick with it.

'I know you don't want the past dragged up, but there's been another murder in Arrow Lake,' I said to her.

She put the cigarette in an ashtray. 'The same as the last time?'

'Similar. This girl is a cousin of one of the original victims: Angela Kerr.' I sat forward on the leather couch, feeling the material warm.

'Oh, her.' She picked up her cigarette again and took another puff. Sat back in her chair, one arm across her front. A classic pose of being hacked off at something. You didn't need to be an FBI profiler to know what it meant when a woman did that. Go back a few thousand years and you would see men do that, except they were holding shields against their bodies. They were preparing to go into battle.

Trish Morgan was also preparing to go into battle. With me.

'You knew Angela?' I asked her, wishing now that I'd accepted the offer of a drink.

'Yes, I knew her. Knew *of* her.' More sucking on the cigarette, blowing the smoke hard. Then she put it down again. Now we were advancing in our fight. She was going to let me have it.

'She had an affair with Tom, the bitch,' Trish said, firing the first salvo.

'Did you tell the investigators this at the time?' I knew she had. I'd read the report.

'Yes. It was one of the reasons they suspected him, if you remember. You were there, you should know.'

'You're right, I remember now.' I didn't want her to think I knew too much or else she might leave something out, assuming I already knew the answer. 'I asked you then and I'm going to ask you again; do you think Tom was guilty of the crimes that were committed?'

'I did back then. It was such a hard time; the girls were bullied at school. I couldn't walk down the street without somebody whispering and pointing: *there's the killer's wife*. It was that hard, we had to move down here, with my mum and dad.'

'Do people know who you are here?' I asked her.

'Not so much. If they do, they don't give us a hard time. But I changed our names. That helps.'

'Were you sure Tom was having an affair with Angela?'

'I couldn't prove it, but somebody told me. I wasn't surprised to be honest. He had fooled around on me years before, when he was with the NYPD. We lived up in Washingtonville at the time, in Orange County. Do you know it?'

'I do. Where the Brotherhood Winery is,' I told her.

'That's it. He travelled down here every day he was working. He was in the 47th Precinct in the Bronx. He loved it, but he was such a distance away. I've seen him stay overnight in a cheap motel when the snow hit hard, instead of him trying to get home. He admitted he had shared a room with a female officer one night. He tried to tell me nothing went on, but I didn't believe him.'

'Is that what caused your marriage to hit the rocks?' I asked her.

'No. It got back to me he was fooling around with a nurse from Mercy University Hospital, not far from his precinct. This one he did admit to. He met her in a club downtown when he and his friends would go out on a boys' night out.'

'You wouldn't know her name by any chance, would you?'

'No. But it was shortly after that we decided that we were either going to give our marriage a go or call it a day. Tom said he wanted to start fresh, and he had heard through his work that they were looking for officers in Arrow Lake. It seemed perfect. Except there's a hospital there, and where there's a hospital, there are nurses, and as you know, Tom liked a bit of nurse to himself.

'We had been there six months when I saw the signs again; staying out late, me answering the phone and nobody there. He denied it of course, but it went on for a while. And then Angela went missing. He was questioned of course but he had an alibi: me.'

Now that I had been inside the house for a little while, I could feel the effects of the air con unit, but still I felt the hairs go up on the back of my neck.

'You alibied him, and I'm having a guess here, but it was false, wasn't it?'

She nodded. I had seen this happen before, the partner of a killer giving him an alibi, even although the woman knew it was a lie, either through fear or misplaced loyalty. By doing that, they had given some innocent woman a death sentence.

She smoked in silence for less than a minute. I waited patiently. 'Look, my marriage was fragile. We were in a strange town now, miles from home. The girls were settled in school, we were putting down roots. I didn't want my marriage to go south. I didn't want to believe he was fooling around with Angela, so I told Chief Walker that Tom was with me that night Angela went missing. It wasn't true. I lied, then I found out he *did* have an affair with her.'

If Morgan had indeed been the killer, then this woman in front of me had given him the ticket to go out and abduct Jessie. I held onto the idea that Morgan was innocent, that some other monster had taken my partner.

'That must have been hard for you to admit that, so thank you.'

'It didn't do any good because other women went missing and he'd been seen out so I couldn't alibi him. *Wouldn't* alibi him. That's when he became a suspect.'

She sucked in more of the cigarette. 'Do you think this latest murder is connected to the murders four years ago? I mean, I know you said it was Angela's cousin, but... you know...'

'I think there is a chance.'

'Do you think Tom was innocent?'

There was a brightness in her eyes now, some glimmer of hope that the man she had shared a bed with wasn't capable of doing the things they had said he did.

'I'm not sure right now. It's a possibility, or it could be a copycat.'

It seemed to be enough for her. 'I knew it. I knew he wasn't a murderer.' She smiled at me as the tears came. 'You'll find this killer, won't you?'

'I'm doing everything I can to do just that.' The stock answer. Feed them enough hope without promising the earth.

'Let me ask you though, when you moved to Arrow Lake, did he ever come back down here? For a visit or anything?'

'Yes,' she answered without hesitation. 'His folks lived in the Bronx, not far from his precinct. He would come down to see them, go out with his old friends and stay overnight. Is that important?'

'I'm not sure yet. It could go towards proving him innocent.' *Or proving he was indeed our killer back then.*

'Thank you,' she said, standing up. I stood up and she gave me a hug. I smelled cigarette smoke in her hair as I put my arms around her. This was probably the first time in years she didn't feel like she'd been stabbed in the heart.

I stepped back into the sunshine, promising her I'd keep in touch and giving her a piece of paper with my cell number on it.

She held it like it was the winning lottery ticket.

TWENTY-ONE

I took the Sprain Brook Parkway then joined the Taconic, heading north. The Taconic was a great road in Westchester, where the taxes were high, then it became a two-lane road with a bad surface, further north. Luckily I was only on the decent three-lane stretch before getting off, heading towards Mohegan Lake.

Pete Sullivan had worked in the Washington office when I first met him. An older, seasoned agent, he had transferred to the BAU a few weeks before I had and we had hit it off, despite the more than twenty-five-year age gap. We'd had drinks on many an occasion, and I had danced at his daughter's wedding and stood by his side as his wife had been lowered into her grave.

I felt a pang of guilt as I drove up Route 6 towards the diner he now owned. I hadn't been in touch for a while. Part of me tried saying it was because of the investigation jobs I took on, coupled with the teaching at the college, but if I was to dig deep and tell myself the truth, I would tell myself I was embarrassed.

I had failed as an agent, not only to hunt down the killer, but to protect my partner. But now I wanted to bite the bullet and go for a coffee. I hadn't called ahead this time. So I could chicken out at the last minute.

The diner looked like a small restaurant, sitting on its own. I parked in a space on the side and walked up the ramp into the building. It was busy, even way after lunchtime. Servers bustled about and a woman smiled at me from the reception counter.

'Table for one, sir?'

'Make that a table for two, Sarah,' Pete said, walking over to me. We shook hands and it felt good to see him again. 'You should have let me know you were coming,' he said, smiling.

'I was just passing and I thought—'

'No you weren't,' he said, laughing softly. 'You're not the only retired profiler, Scott.' He led me over to a table and indicated for a server to come over. We ordered a couple of seltzers and I realized just how hungry I was. I ordered a grilled cheese with fries.

'Tell me, what are you really doing down here?' Pete said. He was looking good, had lost weight, looked like he worked out. He didn't look like he was in his late-fifties.

'He's back, Pete.'

That's all I needed to say. He understood what I meant.

'Why are you down here?'

'The first victim who was put on display, isn't one of the original ones. She was a listed misper, from the Bronx.'

He sat silently for a moment, taking it in. 'That's a whole new ball game. Something we didn't see coming. That means—'

'There could be a lot more that we don't know about,' I said.

'You might not know until he displays more.'

'There have only been two that he's displayed, but he's taken it to a new level – he's started killing again. The victim was related to one of the first victims, Angela Kerr. Tom Morgan was having an affair with Angela.'

'With Morgan being dead, you have the job of finding out who found the bodies.'

The server, a young woman with a smile that said she either enjoyed her job or was faking it for the boss, came with the order. We thanked her and she left. I tucked into the grilled cheese. It was fabulous.

'There's more than one of them,' I said, forking one of my fries. 'You do good food here.'

'Taste's even better when it's on the house,' Pete said, grinning and taking a sip of his seltzer. 'How do you know there's more than one?'

'Just the logistics. They took one of those golf buggies with the small dump truck on the back. Greenkeepers use them. Then the body was carried through the woods from a public path. Maybe I'm wrong. It isn't an exact science after all, but they want my opinion up there and that's my opinion. Plus, Dani's neighbor's dog was alerted by somebody running through the yard, then a second one came crashing through the woods with a mask on.'

'Danny? This the guy you're helping?'

'No, *Dani*, short for *Danielle*. The detective I told you about after I went back a year later. She was a patrol officer when we worked the case.' I ate more fries after finishing the grilled cheese.

'Oh, that Dani. The one you've got the hots for?'

I stopped chewing and looked at him. 'Why do you think that?'

He grinned. 'Again, experience. She was involved in the case, wanting to become a detective, and she was always hanging around us. She had the hots for you back then.'

'I didn't notice.'

'Liar. You still have a lot to learn before you can pull the wool over my eyes.'

'She's a nice woman. And I just spent some time with her ex. He's a cop. NYPD.'

'Scoping out the competition?'

'Hardly. He's just back from honeymoon. Anyway, Dani asked him to take me to speak to Sofia Martinez's parents after they were given the death notice.'

'They'll be shocked to find out their daughter was taken upstate and murdered.'

'They are, but after hearing what they had to say, I'm not surprised now.' I finished the food. 'Let me ask you something. After the murders in Arrow Lake, I was medically retired and you took a transfer to Manhattan. Do you remember there being many missing young women?'

'There were a few. They're mostly dealt with at police level, but we were brought in on a few cases. I can't specifically remember names though, Scott.'

We sat in silence for a moment. 'Do you still think the same way we did back then?' I asked him.

'That Tom Morgan wasn't responsible for the murders? Yes, I do. I stand by that. Nobody wanted to hear it though. That's why I transferred out of Quantico.'

'And why I took the medical pension. What was

the point working for a department who wasn't going to listen?'

'I agree. But let me ask you, do you think that this is the same killer?'

I took a deep breath before answering and let it out slowly. 'I do. We both know what Morgan looked like, and I swear this was a bigger guy who shot me. The suits upstairs said I was mistaken, either through shock, or having blood running down my face, and they almost convinced me I was wrong, but the more I think about it, the more I know I was right.'

'Let's play devil's advocate. Why do you think the authorities up there think he's guilty? And what would the catalyst have been for him to start killing?'

'Okay then, let's start with the reason he was made a suspect: a phone call. An anonymous tip. Somebody saw him with one of the victims, Angela Kerr. I've just spoken to his widow. She told me he had an affair with Angela Kerr. But she lied and alibied him. Later, he couldn't account for his whereabouts when the other victims were taken. How many of the other victims did he have an affair with?'

'Listening to that, I would find him guilty if I was sitting on a jury.' Pete sat back in the booth.

'I agree. She told me they lived in Washingtonville, about half an hour from me. He commuted to work but there were times when he stayed overnight when the weather was bad, or when the boys were having a night out. Now, we know that police officers come into close contact with nurses a lot. What if he met Sofia Martinez when she was on duty? Got chatting to her and arranged to meet up in the nightclub?'

'Nobody would necessarily know him, none of her friends I mean. So she could be having a drink with him, and it would be plausible she left with him.'

'Correct,' I said. 'He had moved up to Arrow Lake only a couple of months before. And his wife told me that he came back down to see his parents and have a night out with some friends of his. It isn't too much of a stretch to think he could have picked up Sofia, given her some story, then killed her and took her back home. Witnesses say she was friendly with the guy, like she was comfortable around him.'

Pete suddenly started to look serious. 'For somebody who thinks Morgan was innocent, you're certainly building a case against him.'

'That's the thing though, Pete, this is all supposition. A *What if?* Sofia knew her killer, I'm convinced of that, so if it wasn't Tom Morgan, who was it?'

'Despite all that, I still think he was railroaded.'

'His wife did a stupid thing by giving him the alibi.'

'If anything, it made him look even more guilty,' Pete said. 'But she couldn't alibi him the other times, because she wasn't with him. He'd been seen out with other women.'

'I think things were getting out of hand. The killer had abducted the women and decided to take the heat off himself and set up Morgan to take the fall. The question now is, why did he keep the bodies hidden for all this time?'

'And what's making him move them? Find out why a cache of bodies that was so well hidden for four years now suddenly has to be moved, and you'll be halfway to finding him, Scott.'

There was something buzzing about inside my head, but it was like a fly that didn't want to land.

'You going back up to Arrow Lake tonight?' Pete asked.

'It's been a long day. I'm going back to my place in Newburgh, then I'll head up in the morning.' I took my wallet out.

'On the house,' Pete said.

'Thanks, but I'll leave something for the server.' I took out some notes and left them on the table for her. We slid out of the booth and stood up.

'Don't be a stranger,' Pete said, shaking my hand. 'Maybe come back and bring Dani with you.'

'She lives far away, Pete.'

He raised his eyebrows. 'Again...'

I held up a hand and smiled. 'I'll bring her down sometime.'

'That's my boy.' He slapped me on the arm and I left the diner. I made a promise to myself that I would indeed bring Dani down one day.

I got in the rental and hit the dial button on the steering wheel. I shocked myself by realizing I was missing her. *You're colleagues* I reminded myself, but then I thought of the nights I'd spent with her. My feelings for her were getting stronger, or maybe it was just two people who had survived a disaster and were now bonding.

'Dani?' I said when she answered. 'How's Atticus?'

'I'm fine, Marshall, and thanks for asking,' she answered, laughing. 'He's fine. Having a ball with my dad. My mum's away to her overnight stay with one of the patients she volunteers for, so my dad is having a blast with your dog.'

Our dog, I thought. *Maybe one day.*

'I'm sure they're having fun.'

'Dad wants me to have Atticus overnight. He forgets I'm a police officer with a firearm, but he wants me to have Atticus with me at night.'

'I can't argue with that,' I said.

'You look after yourself too, Scott. I mean that.'

'I'll be fine here, don't worry. But tell your mom and dad to be aware too.'

'I'll lecture Dad when I get the dog, but Mom can't get a reception for her phone. The woman she visits lives up in the mountains. My mom's only there for a couple of days, then the caregiver comes back. She'll be home before we know it.'

I told her about my plans to stay overnight in Newburgh and how I'd got on with Eddie, her ex. 'Okay. I'll be back at my place in an hour, then I'll leave early tomorrow.'

'Call me before you do.'

'I will.' Turned out I'd be calling her a lot sooner than the next morning.

TWENTY-TWO

'Scott and I were thinking of going up to the cabin,' Dani said to her father.

'Too late. We have to hand over the keys. Tomorrow.'

'Okay. Maybe we could still go out on the boat. You and Mom could come too.' They were sitting in the living room with a log fire burning, staving off the chill summer air.

Bill looked down at the glass of whiskey in his hand and took a sip of it.

'What's wrong, Dad?'

He hesitated before looking at her. 'I'm just being a stupid old man, but I see the way Scott looks at you; the way I used to look at your mother when I was dating her. You were only two when I married her.'

'He's a colleague. We're not dating.' She smiled at

him. 'I can't remember my mother, but Sylvia has been like my own mother. I hope my next marriage is as happy as your second one.'

'Well, it made me think, we've been married for twenty-eight years next month, but by then, the cabin will belong to Magnus Porter, so I asked your mother to join me tonight for a bit of supper up there. She's going there from the old woman's place in the mountain and we'll share some food and a bottle of wine. Spend the night as well. Maybe I'll get lucky.'

'Dad, that is something a daughter does not want to hear.'

Bill laughed. 'I've been thinking that we were heading for getting stuck in a rut, and I don't want that happening. This will be a nice little romantic date for me and your mom.'

'I'm pleased for you.'

Bill took on a serious look. 'Now, tell me to mind my own business, but do you think that you could see yourself going out with Scott?'

Dani didn't hesitate. 'Yes. Three years ago, we spent six weeks looking for any sign of Jessie and I got to know him well. I always thought about him, but neither of us pursued it. Now that he's back here, I feel like I don't want him to go back to Newburgh.'

'Well, follow your heart, honey.'

He grabbed his jacket and walked out. Dani got a hold of Atticus and took him home.

Zach Porter finished his dinner and sat watching his two little girls playing on the carpet in front of him. They were getting in front of the TV but he didn't mind. They would be grown up before he knew it.

'Would you like a beer?' his wife asked him.

'No. I have to go out again.'

'Again? I thought we could sit and watch some TV together.'

He looked at her like she was demented. 'Watch TV together? Are you bored or something?'

She shrugged. 'I just thought it would be nice.'

'Well, as much as I would like to sit and watch some drivel on TV, I have work to do.'

'Why can't they have somebody else go in?'

He stood up, feeling the anger rise. 'Because they don't trust anybody else. They call me in because I know how to do the job.' He shook his head, feeling his face redden. 'Where do you think all this stuff comes from? Me, that's where! I'm the one who works hard while you sit around all day.'

'I'm looking after two kids. Why don't you try it one day? You'll see it's no picnic.'

'You'd like that, wouldn't you?' He smiled at the little girls before turning back to his wife. 'See what you've done? You're upsetting the girls. Just be quiet now.' He grabbed his jacket and left the house.

Soon, the feeling of anger subsided to be replaced by one of ecstasy. The excitement rose through his body like his blood was on fire.

He drove the Jeep away quietly, feeling the rush of excitement. He had more killing to do.

TWENTY-THREE

Bill Fox drove round the north side of the lake where the cabins were. It was full dark now, and chilly. He had thought they could maybe sit out on the deck for a while but it might be too cold for Sylvia. His wife didn't like the cold. He had an idea how to keep her warm though. He grinned at the thought.

He was going to miss the cabin, but he had promised Sylvia they would look for a new one, although he thought he might have to take a part-time job just to pay for it. This cabin had been in the family for years, and it needed some fixing up. Nothing major, but it would have meant spending money on it.

Magnus Porter's company had offered them way over market value for it and he didn't know one person who hadn't accepted the offer. He had to admit he envied the future owners of this lot, having a nice big house here, with views right over the lake.

Life moved on though, and Bill was always one to move with the times.

He pulled his car in front of the cabin. Sylvia's car wasn't here but he knew she was on her way down. He would make a start on the steaks he had brought with him. She was expecting a light supper but he was doing the works.

He took the bags from the truck and walked up to the front door. Crickets made their nocturnal noise from the bushes and undergrowth. It was a soothing noise that he had always liked since he was a boy. When he and his family came here, they used to have so much fun in the summer.

He let himself in, switching on the lights. The heating was on and it made the cabin feel welcoming. He was going to miss the old place.

He put the bags on the kitchen counter and was about to put the bottle of wine in the fridge when he heard the noise coming from upstairs.

Maybe Sylvia was here after all. But where was her car?

'Sil? Is that you, honey?' He walked out to the hallway and stood at the bottom of the stairs. Maybe it was just the old house settling. It was older than him, after all. He walked through to the living room and got the log fired started. They could sit here after their supper and watch the flames.

He thought he heard a creak on the stairs. He picked up a poker and walked through as quietly as he could, holding the tool like a weapon.

Nobody there.

'Everybody is on edge because of this killer,' he said under his breath. He decided to call his wife. Maybe her phone would pick up a signal by now.

He dialed the number and froze, fear gripping him like a steel hand.

Sylvia's phone was ringing, the sound coming from the dining room off the back of the living room. He walked through, his legs feeling like they weighed a ton.

He saw the phone sitting on the table, its screen lit up. He took the phone away from his ear as a voice told him to leave a message.

Too late, he realized the figure was right behind him. Something hard hit him on the head and everything went dark.

TWENTY-FOUR

Sleep eluded me. It wasn't because I was missing having Atticus near me, but the whole house felt like it was a strange place. I was used to having Maria downstairs. Just knowing there was another human being in the house made everything seem... *normal*.

I missed Dani. It felt good to share my life with a woman again, even if it was only going to be for a little while. I knew then that I wanted more.

I lay in bed and thought about three years ago when I had gone back up to Arrow Lake and asked a newly promoted detective for some help. Chief Walker said he could spare Dani for a little while. Turns out she had spent a lot of time with me, six weeks in total.

It had almost been like we were dating then one of us was going off to college, which in a way it was; I had decided to take up the teaching post I'd been offered at

the college. Of course, I would still do private investigation work, but I would fit them in between lectures. I
promised Dani I would keep in touch, which I did, but
then it fizzled away. She had her life and I had mine,
such as it was. I had asked her to come back to
Newburgh with me, but she said she wasn't ready for
that.

I had gone to see a therapist, who gave me what she
called a mental toolbox, to deal with the feelings of
guilt, anger, and despair. There were still times even
now when I felt an almost overwhelming sadness at
having let Jessie down. I wished I could turn the clock
back, but that is a dangerous road to travel down. You
could drive yourself insane by coming up with alterna-
tive scenarios that could never be reality.

I'd promised Dani I would go back up and see her,
but I never had. Maybe it was the feeling of anger that
I got when I thought of going back to that town and
coming away empty-handed that stopped me. I'd
thought that Tom Morgan was a coward, but then the
thought that he wasn't the killer flooded my brain with
unwelcome thoughts.

The big one, the jackpot prize was: *If it wasn't Tom
Morgan, then who was it?* I had constantly scoured the
local paper from Arrow Lake online, and there was
never any mention of women going missing again.

I slept fitfully for a little while. It was a strange

feeling I had, but I was missing Dani more than anything. I got up and went through to the computer. I had to put my investigator hat on. This case wasn't going to be solved the way we were heading into it. I had to start thinking outside the box. There was something sticking right there and I just had to reach out and grab a hold of it.

I started searching, sure I would find our killer just waiting to jump out at me.

I worked until four, grabbed a couple of hours sleep and made a coffee in my Yeti cup.

I had found something that might be news to Dani, but then I thought, maybe it wasn't news.

Maybe it was just a well-kept family secret.

TWENTY-FIVE

The three-hour journey was made in two and a half hours. It was another warm day, and the traffic was starting to build up on I87 north.

Tourists were out in force by the time I hit Arrow Lake. I saw a couple of patrol officers I knew, standing talking to somebody on the sidewalk. There wasn't a sense of fear, not yet. Somebody had been murdered, and a dead body had appeared from four years ago. Nothing to worry about. Yet.

I made it to Dani's house ten minutes later and was mauled by a German Shepherd who thought I'd been away for a year. When he settled down, I gave Dani a hug and kissed her.

'I missed you,' she said, holding onto me.

'It was one night.'

'One night too many.'

After holding each other for a moment, we moved apart.

'What did you find out?' she asked me.

'It's a long story. Are we taking Atticus to your mom and dad?'

'Yes. They were spending the last night at the cabin.'

'Last night?' I said.

'Yesterday was the last day they officially owned it. They have to hand over the keys today, so Magnus Porter can bulldoze it for his new houses.'

'It's going to be a sad day.'

'I said we would drive up and have a coffee with them. I want to look at the place one last time.'

'When are we going?'

She looked at her watch. 'It's almost nine, so they've probably been up for a couple of hours, so we can go now.'

I refilled my Yeti and we took Atticus out to the car. The dog had greeted me and he was now more interested in me throwing a ball, which I did, into the back of the Tahoe.

'I spoke to the Martinez family. Sofia had a stalker. Nothing came of it, but somebody had romantic intentions, though it never played out. But she worked in Mercy University Hospital in the Bronx, not far from where she lived. Not far from Tom Morgan's precinct either. A lot of police officers come into contact with nurses. It's possible that he came into contact with Sofia at some point. He could have met her at the club that night, then driven back here. His widow told me he would sometimes go down to Manhattan to hang out with some old buddies and they would go drinking.'

'He had the opportunity to abduct her. Everything still points to him, but if he didn't do it, then who did?'

'I'm not exactly sure,' I told her. An idea was spinning around in my head, but it wasn't something that I could talk about at that moment. I didn't want to go jumping in with both feet.

Which was just as well. After what we found up at the cabin.

Dani parked next to her dad's car but Atticus was standing in the back of the big SUV, growling. I looked at Dani before turning to the dog.

'What's wrong, boy?'

He barked and growled some more.

We got out of the car, Atticus pulling on his leash. 'Easy,' I told him, but he was still eager to get into the cabin.

Dani took out her phone and called her dad's phone. No answer. Same with her mom's.

'Something's not right,' she said, trying the door

handle on the front door. It was unlocked and the door swung open.

We both drew our guns. I didn't want to let Atticus go. I would rather me be shot than him, so I wrapped the leash round my hand tightly and kept him back.

'Dad! Mom!' Dani shouted as we entered the hall.

Then the smell hit us both and we looked at each other, knowing.

We walked through to the kitchen and we found Bill. He was dead, that was clear.

So were the other two women sitting at the table with him.

TWENTY-SIX

I was standing down by the lake, watching the sun glint off the water. Two people on jet skis were having fun in the distance, unaware of what was going on over here.

There was a buzz of activity from behind me. The subdued noise of radio chatter from the patrol officers.

'You okay?' Nikki Hunter said, coming up behind me and putting a hand on my shoulder.

'I'm fine. It's Dani I'm worried about.' I turned round to see her sitting at the back of the ambulance, a blanket round her shoulders. Atticus was looking at her too, as if he wanted to go over and be with her.

'It must have been horrendous coming in to find her father had killed himself,' Nikki said.

'It was. And finding the other victims.'

'That makes it four from the list of women

abducted from four years ago. Two found back then, Patti Ross and Brittany Lowe. Which started this whole case rolling. Angela Kerr makes three. Two now and one still missing. Six out of the list of six. Plus Sofia Martinez and your partner. The two women at Bill's table are Ellen Wood and Alice Neil, according to the note he left.'

'That leaves Donna Taylor, one of the original victims, still missing. And Jessie.'

We stood in silence for a moment, a quiet breeze coming in off the lake. 'Nobody had any clue that Bill Fox was a serial killer.' I said it out loud more to myself than to her.

She shifted her position and rubbed Atticus's head, just below his ear where he liked it. 'Where were you last night, Scott?' she said quietly. 'Sorry, I have to ask.'

'Don't be sorry. You're the chief of police. It's your job, and a question your detectives will no doubt ask again when they have us in an interview room.' I turned to face her. 'I was at home. At my house down in Newburgh.'

She nodded. 'Good. Your phone records will help prove that, when they show it pinging off the cell phone towers.'

'Sure.' I felt a sense of relief that modern technology could place me three hours away. 'Did Chief Walker suspect Bill?'

'My dad didn't mention Bill by name, but he thought it was a doctor. He didn't say why. The night I was supposed to meet him, he was killed by the driver. And I never found any evidence in his files to support that.'

'He was right, your dad. It is a doctor, not Tom Morgan.'

'Listen, Scott—'

'I know what you're thinking. Here we have a detective and an ex-FBI agent, both of them experienced in investigating murder, one of them more than the other. We would know how to stage a scene, and make it look like the murderer took his own life. But we didn't. I slept alone at my house, nobody saw me to speak to me. I could have driven up through the night and Dani and I, or me by myself, could have killed Bill and placed the corpses to be found. But I didn't. If that's going to be your train of thought, then the killer is going to get away with it.'

'I'm keeping an open mind just now. But it would seem that the bodies were hidden in the other little cabin all these years. It's a wonder they didn't smell.'

'It's a little one-room cabin that held a few extra beds,' I explained to Nikki. 'Sometimes they had parties and there wasn't enough room, so some guests stayed in what Bill laughingly called the overflow lodge. It had a dank, cellar with a dirt floor. It's a place

I never went, and I don't think they've had a big party in the past few years, from what Dani told me. So nobody would have gone in there.'

'Yeah, it looks as if the bodies had been buried in there. I suppose nobody would smell them if they were in the ground in the cellar.'

'If Bill was the killer, then he knew yesterday was the last day they owned it and he would have to get rid of them,' I said.

'Why would they even display a victim to have the case reopened?' Nikki said. 'He would just be drawing attention to himself. I mean, I understand that the cabin and the land were sold, so the bodies would have been discovered anyway, but why didn't they take them and dump them somewhere else?'

'By doing it this way, he was controlling the situation. Being a part of it, in a way.'

'But why would he kill himself?' Nikki said.

'I don't know why,' Dani said, coming up to us.

'I know this is hard, Dani, but do you think your dad was capable of this?' Nikki said.

'No! Of course not. Or at least I didn't think so, until we found him this morning.'

'They found a note. In the basement. It simply says, *Sorry*. And the names of the two victims who were killed four years ago.'

'I can't believe my dad would do this. Abduct

women, then kill them and hide them.' She looked at Nikki. 'When your guys searched the basement, you didn't find my mom, did you?'

'No, but there was some blood on the kitchen floor. There's no obvious cuts on your dad, but it's going to be tested for DNA.'

Dani shook her head, trying to keep her voice from cracking. 'He killed her, took her away somewhere and dumped her.'

'One of the neighbors heard your dad's boat start up and go out late last night. I hate to say it, but he could have taken her out into the middle of the lake and dropped her over. If she's weighed down, she might never be found. It's so deep in the middle that it can't be searched.'

'He loved my mom.'

'Maybe she caught him trying to move the bodies. Maybe he killed her in a fit of rage then decided to display the other bodies.'

I was trying to picture it and couldn't. Dani knew Bill better than I did obviously, but the few times I had met him, he didn't give off any signs that anger could come out of him like that. I couldn't see Bill hurting Sylvia.

'Or maybe it was somebody else.'

Lou Fazio came out of the house, ahead of the coroner's assistants bringing out Bill in a body bag on a gurney. Fazio came over to us.

'I'm sorry about your dad, Dani,' he said.

'Thank you.' Tears rolled down her cheeks.

'And your mom. I mean, I've known Sylvia for ten years. She was the sweetest woman you could meet.'

'Ten years?' I said. 'I thought you'd only worked here for four?'

'Yes, but Sylvia is the Medical Director for the hospital. It's owned by Mercy University Hospital Group. I would often bump into her down in the Bronx. In fact, I think she put in a good word for me to help with my transfer up here. I hope they find her.' He looked at Dani again. 'Anyway, I'm sorry for your loss.' He put a hand on her shoulder and walked away.

'We still have two other victims missing,' I said to Dani, watching Fazio walk away. 'One of the original victims and Jessie Kent, my partner. Where are they?'

Nobody had an answer.

Nobody wanted to say they could be on Bill and Sylvia's other property.

But they were going to look.

TWENTY-SEVEN

There were times when I had been wrong as a profiler. Most of the time, I was right, but there had been times when I walked down one road and I should have been on another.

This was one of those times.

Going out on a limb they called it.

When they were wrapping up at Dani's, I took her aside and I told her I would call her.

I wanted to go to the morgue down at the hospital, run something by Lou Fazio, just not in front of Dani.

I had a feeling I knew why the corpse had been displayed, reopening the case.

I drove down in the Tahoe, leaving Atticus with her and Nikki Hunter.

The van was there and Bill had already been taken out and into the hospital. I went in and through to the morgue. I caught the attention of one of the assistants.

'I'd like a word with Dr Fazio. Is he through in the autopsy suite?'

'No, sir, he got called home on an emergency. He said he'll be back a little later to do the autopsy.'

'Do you know where he lives?'

'Yes.' The girl looked at me.

'Can you tell me where?'

'Sorry, I can't divulge that information.' She smiled like she wasn't sorry at all and walked away.

I knew who would give it to me.

'Nikki? I need a favor. I need Lou Fazio's address. He's not at the hospital but was called home. I want to talk to him about something.'

She hesitated for a second before telling me. I thanked her and headed out.

The drive to where he lived took fifteen minutes from the hospital, heading east out of town. The houses were further apart, and I had to turn into a little-used road, following the directions on the sat nav in the car.

The road ended and a private drive started, going beneath a canopy of trees. The road was rough and dry, throwing up dust. It wound round, deeper into the woods, until I could finally see a house through the trees.

I got to a rough circle at the front of the house. It

was a large property, maybe Victorian. I could see some outbuildings, including a double garage over on the left. The whole property was surrounded by trees. A country getaway for some rich person, back in the day, maybe.

I got out of the car and walked up a few steps to the front porch and knocked on the door. And waited. And waited.

Finally, Lou Fazio opened the door.

'Scott. Everything okay?'

'It's fine, Lou. I hope you don't mind me coming here. I went to the hospital but they said you had a family emergency.'

'Yeah, I just said that. It always sounds better. I just had something to do, that's all. Busy day ahead. It's not every day you get to open up a serial killer.'

'I bet that's the exact same thing that Bill thought, four years ago,' I said, 'since he was the medical examiner back then. But maybe not, since he was really the serial killer.'

He stood looking at me for a moment. 'Is that what you wanted to say, Scott?'

'No. Can I come in for a moment?'

He hesitated again before standing back and opening the door. I stepped into a hallway that was dark, with dark wood trim. It smelled of polish with a hint of something very old. A staircase was over on the left. Also painted dark brown.

The door shut behind me.

'Come through to the kitchen.'

We walked down a narrow hallway into a kitchen that was bright and modern. It turned to the left where a large refrigerator stood.

'Scott, grab a soda and I'll join you in a minute. I have a fax coming through in my home office.'

I waited until he had left the kitchen, opened the refrigerator door slightly, and then shut it again without taking anything out or taking my eyes off the doorway.

I didn't hear anything churning out of a fax machine and wondered if Lou had his office upstairs. I stepped back from the doorway out of habit. I wanted to look out down into the hallway but I didn't want anybody jumping out. A split-second could save your life if you only thought about it.

Nobody was there. No sounds of anybody doing anything. I started walking back down the hallway. It was gloomy, like curtains had been pulled shut in the front rooms.

Then I saw it. A doorway under the stairs. Traditionally a basement door. It was just slightly ajar, just a fraction, so if you were in a hurry and not looking properly, you would miss it.

I gently pulled on the handle, waiting to see if it squeaked or not, my other hand on the gun at my side.

The door opened without a squeak. There was a light on downstairs, a dim glow filtering up to the top of the stairs.

I started making my way down.

TWENTY-EIGHT

I placed my weight carefully on each step as I descended, the light getting brighter the further I got down. I expected a musty smell, and to see a dingy basement where old things were kept, now no longer used by children who had grown up, and old tools hanging on the wall, their last project completed before succumbing to rust and cobwebs.

I turned the corner and there were a few more stairs that led to a door that was also ajar. I pushed it open.

What confronted me was a total and utter surprise.

The basement was clean, carpeted, and was like many a basement apartment I had seen before. I kept my hand on the gun as I entered. There was a living room, furnished sparsely, and the first thing I noticed was the TV was old.

I took in a deep breath through my nose, wondering if I would smell what I thought I might smell: death. But it was clean and fresh-smelling.

There were two doors at the other end of the room. I could hear muffled voices. I noticed a door on my right, which was open. I could see it was a bathroom, in darkness. I walked over to the curtains and pulled one gently aside, to let some better light in.

Beyond the glassless window was a brick wall. Right up to the window, as if somebody had bricked it up from the outside.

I took my gun out of the side holster and held it by my side. The time for playing was over. I gently pushed on the door that was slightly ajar. Two children were sitting on a mattress facing me.

I turned around too late. The baseball bat came crashing down on my arm, my gun flying through the air. Pain shot up to my shoulder but I managed to duck out of the way of the second swing of the bat and threw myself down, rolling away from my attacker. More pain shot up my arm.

'Why did you have to come here?' Lou Fazio said.

'You know why I did. It wasn't going to go on forever.'

'You should have left well alone.'

'Not going to happen.' I stood up and he faced me,

a big man with a big bat. The gun was across by the fake window. 'Who are the children?'

He grinned. 'They're mine.'

'You don't have kids.'

'I beg to differ. You just met them.' He stepped towards me. I turned so that I kept facing him. 'I am going to beat you to a pulp, you know that?'

'Why? Aren't you going to shoot me again?'

'I shot you five times, and still you lived. I was expecting to cut you open on the steel table, to help Bill Fox cut you open and take your insides out, but who would have thought? The surgeons saved you. Lucky Scott. That's what they should put on your tombstone, but this time they can add, *but his luck ran out.*

'Why don't you just give up, Lou? They all know Bill didn't kill those women. You did.'

'Even if they suspect it, they can't prove it. I've covered my tracks well. I just need to get rid of you and then carry on the way I was doing.'

'Where's your wife?'

He hesitated for a moment. 'Never you mind.'

'I saw the padlocks on the doors. You keep her down here, don't you?'

'I said shut up!'

Just then, I saw a person at the bottom of the stairs and the other door next to the girl's room flew open and a woman ran out, screaming, jumping on Lou's back. He writhed like a snake and swung her about and I rushed over to grab my gun but he tripped me. Throwing the woman off, he grabbed my gun.

I was lying close to him and I saw an opportunity and took it. I kicked his left knee, hard, on the side and heard the crunch as it gave out.

'See how you like it!' I shouted at him. He fell down screaming but was still holding the gun. He started swinging it towards me and I knew that being shot for a sixth time in four years and living to tell the tale, was too much luck for one man.

Then the figure I'd seen coming down the stairs fired a gun and Fazio's shoulder exploded in a shower of blood. The wife had run in to be with the girls who screamed at the sound of gunfire.

I rolled over and scrambled across on all fours to get my gun.

'Easy, Scott!' Dani said, still pointing her gun at Fazio. I looked at her as she came across towards me. 'You okay?' she asked, keeping the gun trained on the big man.

'My arm hurts like hell, but I'm fine.'

Fazio got up into a sitting position. 'You bitch! You shot me!'

'That's for killing my father.'

'It was nothing personal.'

'I think it was,' I said. 'Go on, tell her.'

'Tell her what?' he sneered.

'Tell her who your mother really is.'

TWENTY-NINE

Fazio stayed silent. I looked at Dani. 'His mother is Sylvia.'

'What? How? I never knew...'

Fazio grinned. 'He's right.'

'Where's my mom?' Dani shouted.

'Not *your* mom, *my* mom! You were only her *step*daughter.'

'Is he telling the truth?'

I nodded. 'Yes. He was adopted but he was Sylvia's son. And Magnus Porter's. They called him Zach Porter before he was put up for adoption.'

'How did she end up meeting him again?'

Fazio stared at Dani with eyes full of hatred. 'I found out who she was. Found out that she worked for the same hospital. She was a surgeon. We connected ten years ago. Then she went into administration, became the Medical Director. She knew her husband was going to retire, and when Bill finally left, I took over from him. We worked together for a couple of months, Bill overseeing things. He didn't know I was Sylvia's son.'

'I don't care. She was my stepmother since I was two years old. I never knew my mother. Sylvia *is* my mother. Tell me where she is!'

'I don't know where she is.'

'Liar! Have you killed her?'

'You two are so smart, you work it out.'

'There were two women in my dad's cabin this morning. That leaves one more, Donna Taylor, and Scott's partner, Jessie. Where are they? What have you done with them? And where's my mother?'

'Questions, questions.'

'The boat went out onto the lake last night,' I said. 'Sorry, Dani, we might never know.'

Her voice was quieter now as the woman brought her kids out, and I got a good look at her now.

'Where's Scott's FBI partner?' Dani shouted at Fazio.

I put a hand on her arm. 'You're looking at her,' I said quietly, nodding towards Fazio's wife. 'Dani, meet Jessie Kent.'

THIRTY

The next five days went by fast. Dani had to arrange Bill's funeral, while the feds had taken Lou Fazio aka Zach Porter to Upstate Correctional Facility, a supermax prison in a little town called Malone, which was spitting distance to the Canadian border.

'He's still not talking,' Dani said, holding onto my arm. 'He won't say where my mom is, or Donna Taylor.

'You have to realize that he might never talk.'

'I know.'

'We live in a state that doesn't have the death penalty, so it's not as if he can plea-deal that away.'

'It still seems unreal that he was our killer four years ago.'

'He just shadowed your dad until your dad retired. He was working away in the background, keeping his eyes and ears open. He befriended Bill, knowing that Sylvia was his mother.'

'Do you think my mom knew who he was?'

'I doubt it. He was just using her. I think he had killed women before he killed Sofia Martinez, but now he was feeding off the notoriety. Maybe he was getting back at his biological father, Magnus Porter.'

'Then why didn't he just leave the bodies there, in my parent's cabin?'

'I have no idea. It seemed he was sticking the finger up to your mom by putting the bodies there.'

We walked towards her car in the sunshine. It seemed like it was too nice a day for a funeral. 'I'll never stop hoping she's found, but from the witness accounts, there's no doubt Fazio took my dad's boat out, and there's more than a good chance he dumped my mom in the lake. Just to punish her. I'll never stop loving her, but I think it's time to move on.'

I was going to get in the car. Somebody from the K9 unit was looking after Atticus for us and I was anxious to get back to him. Dani stopped me.

'I want to show you something,' she said.

We walked along the track a bit more, then moved in a few rows. Dani stopped in front of a grave.

'You asked me to come down to Newburgh three years ago. I told you I wasn't ready. He's the reason I wasn't ready.'

I read the name: *Charles Fox. Died in infancy.*

'He lived for a month and a day. I got to hold Charlie before he had to go. My little boy.' She turned to me with tears running down her cheeks. 'It was the reason Eddie and I split up. Not because he was fooling around on me, but because our little boy died, and I was just so angry, that I blamed him for everything.'

I hugged her.

'So you see, Scott, I wasn't ready to leave my little boy three years ago. But now I can. My dad's here and he can look after him. They're not far apart. Does that make sense?'

'Perfectly.'

'I'd like to go home now. I can't wait to go home to Newburgh.'

We walked back to the car.

'What's going to happen to Jessie?' she asked as I started the car up.

'She'll get therapy and help with the girls. He repeatedly raped her and kept her there and she got pregnant, twice, and he said he'd kill the children if she ever tried to escape. She'll get all the help from the bureau she needs. After all, she's still an FBI agent.'

'Will you see her before you go home?'

'I will.'

'Just a few more days, so I can get my house on the

market and wrap things up here and I can come down. With our dog.'

I smiled. He certainly was our dog, and it was going to be good for us all to be together.

I drove out of the cemetery.

THIRTY-ONE

I left the next day. I called Maria to give her a heads-up about Dani moving down and she was delighted. I told her there was no need to rush back and to spend some more time with her family. Family was important.

I felt a sense of relief and excitement. I couldn't believe we'd got Jessie back. I'd always imagined finding her corpse and putting her into a box, standing at the graveside with her family by my side.

I'd spoken to her father. Her mother had passed away, never knowing that her daughter was still alive. Her father was glad I'd called. He'd do anything to help his daughter, and now two granddaughters.

Then the feeling of guilt hit me again. If I had gone out with her that night, she would have still been a working agent. Now, her career was no more, but she would still get all the support she needed.

Chief Walker had told Nikki Hunter that he suspected the killer was a doctor. I still didn't know why he had come to that conclusion. Maybe something Fazio had let slip? His mistake had not been voicing the name, but maybe he'd feared ridicule.

Two of the victims propped up at Bill's dining table were Patti Ross and Brittany Lowe. Two innocent women whose lives had been snuffed out by an egomaniac. Both of them nurses. That had been Fazio's thing, taking nurses. That just left one original victim unaccounted for, Donna Taylor.

Where was she? Why hadn't Fazio displayed her too? Why just the other two women when he was trying to frame Bill?

I figured he dumped Dani's mother in the lake for two reasons; she wasn't part of the plan so burying her didn't fit in with his plan. Most serial killers stuck to an MO, and Sylvia wasn't in the right age range and not part of the scheme.

The fact that she was his mother didn't bother him. He was taking her away from Dani after all.

I parked the rental car outside the front of the house. There was a basement entrance round the back, but that was the entrance to Maria's apartment, and I always entered through my front door. Although she was my live-in housekeeper, I respected her privacy.

Even though she wasn't home, I still went in the front door.

I walked in, picked up the mail and stepped into the living room.

I could smell it right away. Something not right. Atticus would have known, but he was taking care of Dani.

The living room was on my right and didn't have doors. The doorway on the far side also led into the hall, across from the kitchen. On my left was a bedroom. Nothing unusual in there. My bedroom was straight ahead. The door was ajar. I took my gun out and gently pushed the door. Nothing untoward.

I thought my imagination was getting the better of me. I walked along the hallway, the dividing wall between me and the living room on my right. The door to the basement apartment was on my left. I walked past, to the kitchen. Everything fine. I looked through the door into the small sunroom. Nothing.

I sighed. 'Get a grip of yourself, Scott,' I said, putting my gun away. The house just needed airing out. Or did it?

I walked back into the hall and opened the basement door. The smell hit me. Stronger here. What in the name of God was it?

I put the light on, wondering if Maria had indeed come home early and was surprising me by cooking something but it had gone awry. I didn't shout out. I walked slowly down the stairs and opened the door to her apartment.

There was a short hallway with the laundry room off to the right. Straight ahead was her kitchen.

I could see the lid was off the garbage can, and a clear bag of garbage was almost overflowing. It hadn't been tied and it stank. I put my gun away and walked towards the kitchen and then I saw what the smell was coming from. Too late.

The rotting corpse of Donna Taylor was propped on a chair.

I had figured that Lou Fazio had been working with a partner, but then I'd had my doubts when we caught him. He was big enough to haul corpses on his own, but now that I saw Donna sitting on one of the chair's, I knew I had been right.

Lou Fazio *had* been working with somebody.

And that person was in here with me now.

THIRTY-TWO

The gun was pressed against the back of my head, and a hand took my own gun from the holster I was wearing.

The gun was taken away and I was roughly pushed forward so I couldn't suddenly swing round and fight.

'You didn't see this coming, did you, Scott?' Sylvia Fox said.

The gun was pointed straight at my face, unwavering.

'You got me there,' I said to her.

She smiled, but it was a smile full of evil. 'Isn't this the bit where you ask me to confess? To explain why I did it?'

'I *know* why you did it.'

'Really? Let's hear it then. And sit beside your friend there. You've been wanting to find out what happened to them for four years, now you know. So sit down, or I'll put one through your good knee.'

I sat down and put my hands on the table. Looked up at the clock on the wall in Maria's kitchen.

'Don't be looking at the clock. You're not going anywhere, except straight to hell.' She changed position. 'If you're so smart, tell me how you knew it was me.'

'I didn't *know* it was you. I just let my imagination run riot. After something Lou said. Or do you want me to call him by his first name? Zach.'

She gritted her teeth and took a step forward, straightening her arm out.

I brought my hands up in surrender. 'Okay, Lou it is.' I put my hands back on the table. 'I thought Lou was working with somebody, but I couldn't figure out who it could be. Then I remembered Bill talking about Lou coming up from the Bronx, and to be honest, it wouldn't have stuck in my mind, but you deliberately spilling your drink at the table made that stick. I found out that Tom Morgan had also worked down there and had contact with Sofia Martinez. Of course, we knew he had been NYPD a couple of years before the killings started, but then, we didn't know about Sofia. That connected him, but it also connected Lou. I realized that after Bill mentioned it.'

'He always did have a big mouth.'

'You were a surgeon then you became Medical Director when the Arrow Lake hospital was taken over by the Mercy University Hospital Group. Ten years ago. That's when you first met Lou, according to him. Is that when you found out he was a serial killer?'

'Shortly after that.'

'And that didn't bother you?' I kept my voice even, not wanting to sound condescending.

'No. They were sluts, all of them. Just like the ones at our hospital. Falling over the doctors, and even flirting with Bill when they'd had one too many.'

'Professionals just unwinding after a hard day's work, you mean.'

'I know what I mean.'

I kept my eyes on the gun. 'You were so happy to have your son back in your life, you were willing to not only look the other way, but to help him. But let me ask you, how many did he kill in the past four years since he took Jessie?'

'None that you know about. None from Arrow Lake. I told him he would have to be careful. We'd set up Tom Morgan to take the fall.'

'Then why did you ruin it all by displaying the victims from back then?'

'We'd sold the cabin to old man Porter. I wanted to have the cash for me and Lou to start a new life under new identities. We could be together again.'

'What about Cathy Kerr? That just put *The Gravedigger* on the radar again. Made it look like Tom Morgan had been innocent.'

'That was a mistake. She was snooping. Lou took care of her. It's not what I would have done, but we had to work around it.'

I looked her in the eyes. Saw not madness but something else. 'What about Dani? Where does she fit in here? She's your daughter. You were just going to leave her?'

'She's only my stepdaughter. Yes, I loved her, but Lou is my flesh and blood. You know what it's like, you have a mother. A mother-and-son bond can't be broken, no matter what. Lou means everything to me, and you took him from me.'

I took in a deep breath and let it out slowly. 'I didn't come here alone.'

'Of course you did. I saw you get out of your car. No other cars pulled in.'

'Not at the front.'

She looked past me out of the back window. I was far enough away from her so she couldn't be attacked.

'The old bluff, huh? Trying to divert my attention so you can jump me and take the gun away.' She turned to me and I saw pure hatred in her eyes. 'Let me give you a fair chance. I'm going to kill you, but not with the gun. And remember, I'm fit enough to have helped Lou. I work out. I might seem like some doddering old woman, but you're going to find out the hard way. You thought it was Tom Morgan who shot you four years ago and kicked your knee out.'

'I know it was Lou. He told me.'

She laughed, her face a sneer of contempt. 'Wrong again. I kicked your knee out and shot you. I was going to shoot you in the head with the automatic I had, after I used the revolver. But the gun jammed and I heard shouts. I ran, unjammed the gun and returned fire, but I wasn't close enough to shoot you in the head. I thought you would die anyway. I gave the gun to Lou so he could take care of Morgan in one of the cabins.'

She ejected the shell from the gun and took the magazine out. Laid both items on the kitchen counter. Before I could stand, she moved fast towards me and punched me in the face, knocking me sideways off the chair.

This wasn't the first time I'd been in a fist fight so I rolled and got up on my feet, feeling my right knee crunching. The cartilage had been damaged when Sylvia had kicked my knee out before. It made me a little bit slower in getting up, giving the older woman a chance to kick me in the ribs.

She was right about one thing: she was fit. The kick knocked the wind out of me.

'I think that should be enough, don't you?'

'I don't think so,' Sylvia said, going for a knife in the block on the counter.

'I wasn't talking to you.'

The back door exploded inwards and a second figure ran in from the hallway.

'Drop the knife!' Nikki Hunter shouted from the back door.

'Drop it!' Dani shouted. Both women were holding guns.

Sylvia acted like they weren't even there. She turned towards me as I struggled to get up and raised the knife. The first blow would be a fatal one.

Dani looked at the woman she thought of as her mother and hesitated. Had she been the only one there, I would have died. Again. This time for good.

Nikki had no such qualms. She fired six rounds, the last one hitting Sylvia in the head, killing her instantly.

Dani ran over to me. 'Are you okay?'

'I'm fine.' I didn't mention her hesitation. I looked at Nikki, a look passing between us. *Thank you.*

Dani helped me straighten up.

'You were right,' she said, her voice barely a whisper.

'I wish I'd been wrong,' I said, 'then this would just have been a day trip for you and Nikki. And Atticus playing with the K 9 officer for a day.'

'But you weren't. You said things didn't fit, getting rid of Sylvia, knowing she was his mother and the fact he had somebody helping him.' She looked down at the dead woman. 'She didn't even care about me. She was willing to sacrifice my dad and just walk out of my life and never see me again. The same woman who held my baby son's hand and said he was the most precious thing.'

I held her again. Watched as Nikki made the call.

I held Dani like that until we heard the first sirens.

AFTERWORD

Thank you for reading this Marshall novel. If you could please spare me a couple of minutes to give me a review on Amazon or Goodreads, that would be appreciated. Giving a review to an author like me means we can continue writing the books for you.

I would like to take this opportunity to thank Louise Unsworth Murphy, Wendy Haines, Julie Stott, Fiona and Adrian Jackson, Jeni Bridge, Michelle Barragan, Evelyn Bell, Merrill Astill Blount, Vanessa Kerrs, Bejay Roles and Barbara Bartley. A big thank you to each and every one of you!

Thank you to my wife Debbie, who works away in the background. My daughters, Stephanie and Samantha.

And a big thank you to you, the reader, for joining me on this outing. Without you, it's all for nothing.

'Til next time!

John Carson
New York
March 2019

ABOUT THE AUTHOR

John was born in Edinburgh, Scotland, but now lives in New York State with his American wife and their three children.

He is the author of the DI Frank Miller series, the DCI Harry McNeil series, both set in Edinburgh. He also writes the Max Doyle series of thrillers set in New York, and also the Scott Marshall thrillers set in New York.

www.johncarsonauthor.com

Facebook.com/johncarsonauthor
Twitter.com@johncarsonbooks
Instagram.com/johncarsonauthor

Made in the USA
Monee, IL
04 December 2023

48144651R00142